The Education

of

Twig

LOUISE IRELAND-FREY

A Novella

By Louise Ireland-Frey

Interior Layout & Design by Scribe Freelance
www.scribefreelance.com

ISBN: 978-098-236-6615

FOREWORD

This is not really a children's story. It is an allegory that might have been written about the innocent, ignorant young of any species of being, whether in physical embodiment or not. The little episodes came to me more or less in chronological order and I wrote them down, not planning any plot nor lesson. Afterward I realized that the story did have at least a flow, moving from Twig's original state of dependence and not-knowledge through successive stages of learning and independence, until the stage of responsibility, wisdom, and service to beings was attained.

Thus Twig represents, in twighood, the early stage of any youthful being, whether human or animal or (as in this case) plant. Experience produces increased knowledge and understanding and eventually maturity, wisdom and receptivity to Greater Minds. The maturation is not only in the psychological sense, but also in spiritual expansion. Death of the body is not a major impediment, merely a freeing for further growth, the expansions continuing, from individual, to Bigger, to Still Bigger, toward Biggest. The concept of a Group Spirit for each species or Family of species is not original with me. It occurs in ancient writings, some of which are pre-Buddhistic.

When asked what my source was for this story, I could think only of a few paragraphs in Salten's book, *Bambi* (the original from which Disney made his series). In those few lines two leaves were talking about what it would be like to fall from the branch. "We go down..." But the question remained unanswered, as the last leaf lost its hold and fell free.

Pronouns here are arbitrary, although botanically there are male and female trees in some species. This Tree is probably a poplar or aspen. I didn't really ask. I simply wrote down what "came." So Twig became "he" and Pine Tree became "she." "Moving" became "he" and Earth, of course, was "she." No sexism is intended!

Some symbols are straightforward - "Helper" for the law of Gravity, for instance. Other concepts are straight botany or astronomy. Still others are common but puzzling, like the phantom limbs of Tree after Tree's severe pruning. I asked several friends how Dear Earth's advice should be expressed to help Tree reduce discomfort in the severed limbs. Two friends have had amputations themselves. A third is sensitive to energies and uses energies in her therapy work.

I was asked why I made Twig continue to be childlike. That is just how the story "came," and really Twig should have matured more in his speech habits as he became wiser and more responsible.

Professor Reyes Garcia of the Philosophy Department at Fort Lewis College asked me to talk to a couple of his classes about Twig. The students' questions were penetrating and stimulating. They caught the fact that Twig's tale is an allegory, but when they asked about plot and other literary attributes I had to admit that this writing was not constructed. It isn't *literary*. It "just came."

CONTENTS

THE EDUCATION OF TWIG

___

1. TWIG BEGINS A NEW SEASON

Twig was young and happy. Air was warm and quiet, but Moving was brushing Twig gently from time to time, and the touches made Twig happy, too.

"You, again?" Twig sent the thought outward into Air.

"Yes, just me, Moving," came the answering thought.

"Nice." Twig wafted the cozy pleased feeling out to Moving.

Twig already knew about Touch and Light and Dark. Light was nice; but so was Dark in a different way.

Light was usually filled with little trickles of energies that made Twig feel warm and full of livingness. Dark was usually cool and restful, full of soft Life-urgings from Branch that made Twig feel safe and nourished. Those feelings were in the Light, as well, but during Light times Twig was also more aware of other vibrations and thinking other thoughts - like right now, he was thinking about Moving's touches.

"*Not always nice,*" came a dim thought from Branch.

Branch had in himself memories of other Movings that had been frightening - times when each Leaf and Twig had to depend only on its Union Place with Branch in order to remain attached.

Right now, however, Moving was gentle and peaceable. Branch let the old memories waft softly into and through all its Twigs and then clear out into Distance. They could be recalled fully at any time of need, if Moving began to become obstreperous. Branch waved his twigs gracefully at the suggestions of Moving's repeated pushes. This was a favorite little game they played.

Moving made a quick side-pass through some tall weeds, making them rustle. He nodded into the weeds. That was what he wanted, a chuckling sound to express his feeling of laughter at remembering other times they had played together, he and Tree and the weeds.

Moving himself was changeable and erratic, not like Trees. He pushed into one Tree and its Branches waved in little arcs. As he puffed at another Tree, its Branches remained almost still but each Leaf fluttered and swung vigorously. *Different.* Moving shrugged by turning off to one side and going briefly in another direction.

"Wonder why *different*?" he thought, but let the question waft away into Distance. This lovely quiet day he was content to drift along without aim, just floating and dreaming and remembering... A nice day to be Living.

He drifted above the dry Elm seed-pennies that had fallen from one Tree and now were in piles and rows where Moving had left them

"Well, and it is a nice day to be Not-Living-Till-Later, too," he thought softly.

2. LITTLES INTO BIGS, AND BIGS TO LITTLES

Today Twig leaned into Moving with a happy feeling that something was going to happen - maybe it was already happening. There were feelings of something changing in three places along Twig's length besides a very definite spot at Twig's tip. Something felt like an outward eagerness, a good, spring-like outward pushing. These places tickled, almost.

"What's happening?" he sent the question to Branch. Branch would know; he always did.

"Sprouting," replied Branch briefly.

"Sprouting?" Twig was puzzled.

"Buds, silly."

"Oh, Buds, yes, I remember when I was in my Budhood..." vaguely Twig recalled. Then he relaxed to enjoy this new feeling. The warm trickles of Life-Force from Light and the good nourishing Life-Streams from Branch met together and made a kind of happy little dance of growing, of stretching, of - - Oh, it was complicated and yet simple and nice!

Twig let the new feelings stretch outward at all the tickly places, almost felt the Buds swelling, and felt proud and protective.

"My Buds," was the thought that welled up inside, growing like a Bud itself. Twig knew that the Buds were to him as he was to Branch, really parts of one being. Then for a moment Twig wondered about Branch. Was Branch part of Something Else? This idea had never before occurred to Twig. Now he sent the thought out to Branch.

"Oh, yes, I am part of Big Branch," came the answering thought. "And Big Branch is part of Bigger Branch, and there are many Bigger Branches."

Twig's mind quivered. "I don't understand!" he sent out desperately.

Moving soothed him. "Just natural, Littles to Bigs everywhere," came his quiet thought.

Twig calmed down. Moving knew lots of things, as Branch did. So there were many Big Branches, and even many Bigger Branches? Twig couldn't imagine such immensity. Lots of Twigs, yes, that he could understand. But - - And then another thought occurred to him.

"What about Bigger Branch? All the Bigger Branches?"

"They are all parts of Biggest Branch. Some say that Biggest Branch is the same as Trunk, or even the same as Tree. I guess Tree knows."

"*Tree?*" What is Tree?

"Oh, Tree is the Source of everything, everything except Light and Air. Tree is the Source of our life, our food, everything. There are the three: Tree, and Light, and Air - and Moving is part of Air. For us, that's all there is. The Three are Everything. That is, except for Dear Earth."

Now Twig had really come to the end of his power to understand. For a long moment he remained very still indeed, thinking, until the tickling in his Buds reminded him of today's tasks.

Firmly, and with more serious thought-patterns from the conversation with Branch flowing through his veins outward into the new Buds, he sent them stretching, swelling for tomorrow.

3.   THE WARM TIME BRINGS LEAVES

Tomorrow brightened after the cool dark time, and the Buds were a tiny bit larger already. Twig felt their eagerness as if there were a give-and-take between him and his Buds.

"Yes, just as there is a giving and a receiving between Branch and me," thought Twig. The idea gave him a good feeling of closeness and rightness, of security. "Branch takes care of me and I take care of my Buds," he thought, with satisfaction.

"Just as Tree takes care of all of us," came the thread of thought from Branch.

Twig paused. "You mean that Tree feels about us as I feel about my Buds?

"Of course, silly. How else did you think that Tree would know how to tell each of us which direction to grow, and how to spread our Leaves?"

Twig tried to imagine it. What a huge awareness Tree must have! Well,

7

Branch said that Tree received water from Dear Earth, brought it up through Trunk, and sent it to all the Bigger Branches and common Branches and then into all the Twigs and they into their Buds and Leaves... What a huge affair it all seemed to little Twig!

After a while he decided that he just could not get this whole great idea, so he relaxed against Air, tested the Union Places of all his Buds once more, and then rested. Somehow, after all, he felt safe, cherished, protected.

The days of the Warm Time became days of the Hot Time, and Light from the Bright Direction sometimes came from nearly straight Up. The Light was hot and direct.

The Buds loved it, no matter hot how it felt. They had pushed open their capsules and let the outer scales fill away and go Down, while the inner tender layers seized the yellow and orange vibrations from the Light and drank the juices that Twig was sending them, and each one swelled and spread until from each former Bud there developed a tiny Leaf on a tiny short stem.

Twig was sealed to each one through its Union Place. "My Leaves," he thought, proudly.

During the nights the little Leaves continued to expand slowly. During the days they expanded even faster. Before long they had spread their flat surfaces wide enough for Moving to play with them, twisting them on their stems and making them flutter. Until now their stems had been too short to let them wave and flutter like this, in games with Moving.

Twig had slowly become aware that each Leaf was sending its little individual thoughts to him. At first he had paid small attention, simply sending each one its share of the watery xylem juices that Branch was relaying to him. Now he began to be more clearly aware of the joyfulness of his Leaves, of their little questions, of their enjoyment of their games with Moving...

He began to feel a different kind of relationship to Moving, in fact, as if they both were protectors of the Leaves. He even began to sense the presence of the other Leaves of Branch. They must be quite a bit like his own Leaves, with similar needs, questions, happy feelings. Twig also began to understand more of what Branch felt and knew... He felt himself expanding, not only in girth and length, but in these other ways as well. It was a very good feeling, a strong feeling.

A thought to him from Branch: "Well, Twig, are you *maturing* a little

8

bit?"

"What's *'maturing'*?"

"What you are doing these days, *feeling* that you belong to Tree, like all the rest of us parts of Tree. So when Tree makes decisions to send you growing in a certain direction, you grow that way, knowing that direction is best."

"Why should any direction be better than any other?"

"Oh, if the Bright Direction is hidden by many Leaves so that your own Leaves are shaded from the Light, then you might be told to curve yourself. Well, you may be too stiff for that, but you could turn your Leaves or have them curve their stems, so they can get more Light. See?"

Twig pondered. He had been thinking he had learned so much, yet it seemed that there was always more for him to learn. Once he might have felt overwhelmed, but now this idea just made him more thoughtful.

"So many things to know, so much to learn - but all of it seems wonderful," he decided.

The days and nights of warmth passed quietly in the work of the Leaves. Almost fully expanded, they went to work as soon as Light from the Bright Direction reached them. Taking its energies of yellow and orange and red, they united the breath from Air with the watery xylem sent by Twig and made food from these ingredients. The food, dissolved in more liquid, they sent as rich sap or phloem back into Twig, who passed it on to Branch, who in turn sent it into Bigger Branch, and so on down to Trunk.

Twig felt his own place in this sequence as a small but important part and was content to be just who he was and what he was.

Again he felt that rather amused thought from Branch, "Yes, Twig, you really are *maturing*. Congratulations. Just don't forget that the new Twig growing from you will be very young and uneducated, and be gentle and patient with her. Answer all her questions the best you can before you refer her to Moving or to me."

These thoughts startled Twig. For a moment he was stiff with surprise.

"New Twig? Branch must mean my End-Bud, 'Terminal Bud.' Is she growing now?" He checked, and found that End Bud had indeed begun to show signs of growth, almost hidden at the base of End Leaf's stem. Tuning into her thoughts, Twig found that she had been waiting until all of Twig's first Leaves had spread out before she began to unfurl her own outer Bud-layers.

"I sent you as much water as you asked for," Twig sent his apology to her.

"I wasn't to grow until now, and now only if there is enough water still," she answered.

"Oh, we have plenty of water - for now, anyway," he added, sensing a warning from Branch.

"Yes, so now I am ready to grow," was the contented thought from End-Bud. Twig felt her stretching, and in response sent her an extra thought of approval. She was happy, and so was he! She was his new Twig-part, growing right from his old self, just as he grew from Branch. He felt important and proud.

4.   NOISES, LAUGHTER, AND HEARS TO HEAR WITH

New flavors were coming to Twig through the veins from Branch, and they kept reminding him of what Branch had said about *Tree*.

Twig wanted to see Tree, to feel Tree, to listen while Tree answered questions.

Twig wondered if Moving knew. Moving knew many things because he went so far so easily. Twig was *just right here*, and only went little ways to and fro, or up and down, that's all. But Moving could visit and touch many other Twigs and Branches and things. That's why Moving was so wise.

Right now Moving was calm and still, resting in the Light. Twig felt the good fluids of the sap from Branch nourishing his own slender body and flowing to each of his precious Leaves. In another while the Light would dim into the Between-time, the Warm would become Cool, and Moving would no doubt stir himself and go whispering off somewhere.

After the not-dark of the Between-time there would come the real Dark, sometimes with certain vibrations in Air that came mostly during the Dark: Moving called some of the vibrations "Crickets," and others "Barking," while Branch seemed to lump all of them into *"Sounds."*

These vibrations and many others became more interesting to Twig as he learned to focus outside of himself.

For a long time he had been interested in only his own feelings, thoughts, and the sensations about things that touched him, like Moving and Rain and Light; and then he began to be aware of such vibrations as these of

Sounds.

Now Twig was learning that some Sounds were safe and could be ignored, like Barking, some were nice, like Rain dropping, and some were frightening, like Storm.

When Moving began one of his more obstreperous spells and began to lash and whip things, then Twig strengthened his will, his courage, and especially his Union Place with Branch, and just waited, holding tight to Branch, until Storm went away. These times had come on several occasions, so Twig had became used to them and was not scared at all. He just held on and waited each time.

Sounds during Day time were different from Sounds of the Dark, mostly. Twig thought about Sounds. Branch was calm about them all. When he spoke of certain Sounds as Laughter, Twig asked what that was.

"Laughter is the noise that Children and other creatures make when they are happy."

"Noise?"

"Yes, the vibrations that come with those feelings."

"What is *children*?" Twig sent the puzzled thought to Branch.

"Oh, *children* isn't an IS, it is an ARE: *Children* are the Larvae, the young of *People*."

Twig was learning so many things! He knew through Branch what Larvae are. They are the babies of Beetles. They are born in Branches and eat their way under the bark and itch and feel bad to Branches. But he was perplexed by People. "What is *People*?" he asked.

Branch swayed as Moving pushed him, and sent the rather weary thought, "*People* are the adult forms of *Children*, silly. And they feel Sounds through stick-outs on the head-part. The stick-outs are called *Hears*, because People call feeling the vibrations *Hearing the Sounds*."

Day-sounds were often of whirrings and whizzings. Twig was so accustomed to sensing these that it was with a sort of surprise when one day he realized he didn't know what caused them. It wasn't Moving, for they could continue when Moving was Moveless. He asked Air about these noises.

Air was casual. "Oh, those are from all the Cars going by on the Road."

"What is *Cars*," wondered Twig, "and *Road*?"

"Cars are creatures, quite big ones, that are very calm and quiet ordinarily, but most of them have parasites, poor things. When a parasite gets into a Car, the Car gets agitated and tries to relieve itself of the invader. It rumbles, trembles, makes noises, and runs wildly, but it can't find peace and quietness until it gets rid of the parasite. Then it can be still and rest. And," Air continued, "it is strange, but it seems that the parasites are usually People. I often see a People leave a Car and the Car becomes quiet, whereas when I see a People enter a quiet Car it then becomes noisy and agitated and tries to run away."

Twig absorbed all this new knowledge and it lent new awareness to his sensing of all the rushing and whizzing sounds that reached him. People, he decided, were strange creatures indeed.

The whizzings and rustling usually quieted somewhat in the Dark. Twig continued to nurture his Buds and to receive his nourishment from Branch whether it was Dark or Light, whether there were Sounds or not.

Twig felt happy and safe. It was a pleasant feeling, with eager feelings of growing and stretching, too. And always Air was around him, often ignored but always there.

5.   MOVING AND MOVELESS PARTS OF AIR

That was another things that confused Twig, that Air was always around him but Moving was sometimes touching him and sometimes not, yet Moving said it was part of Air.

"When you aren't playing with me," Twig sent the thought to Moving, "when you aren't touching or pushing me, where do you go?"

"Oh, anywhere I want to, anywhere the Big Movings of Air tell me to go."

"You mean there is a Big Moving, like a Big Branch to Branch?"

"Of course. Bigs to Littles, and Littles to Bigs - that is a kind of law, it seems."

"Is that why sometimes you get so wild and noisy?" asked Twig.

"Yes, I get my orders from Big Moving. That is rather like feeling a half-emptiness, like low-pressing-down on Dear Earth, with other feelings in other places of high-pressing-down. When that happens, I want to Move into that half-emptiness, that low-pressing-down place... You won't understand," he finished with a sigh.

"Well, I try to," countered Twig rather defensively. He felt that Moving was wise but didn't want Moving to remind him of his own lack of knowledge. "A bit conceited," he thought.

Moving felt the thought and sent a humorous, rather tired rejoinder. "It's all right, little Twig. We are all doing what we are supposed to do. I Move, you Grow and put out Buds."

After that last sigh, Moving seemed to vanish. Twig waited, but no longer felt his touch.   "Where are you? Where did you go?" Twig sent out the question into the Air.

There was no reply. Twig sent a more concentrated thought, "Where are you, Moving?"

No response.

Then Twig focused all his energy on a penetrating silent Question: *"Moving? Moving!"*

Again there was no answer, no touch, no thought, no feeling, nothing. Moving was just gone. Twig felt deserted. Why had his friend left him?

Oh, at other times Moving had been gone, too, but somehow there had always been a return, or at least a tiny waft of *reassurance* of return.

Sadly, forlornly, Twig relaxed against the soft support of Air, and somehow Air breathed the reassurance that Twig needed. It was as if Air reminded Twig that *Air* was always here, and that *Moving was indeed part of Air.*

"Moving" was just resting - it was "Moveless" now. Yet the pause seemed very empty to Twig, somehow.

He thought once more to Moving - that is, to Moveless - but again received no reply. He had almost given up hope of feeling his friend again when all of a sudden there was that familiar touch, just a waft of Air, the lightest brush against his side.

"Moving!" he sent the happy thought outward. "Where did you go?"

"Didn't go anywhere. Just stopped moving for a minute. Now I'll be on my way again."

"No, wait, I want to know more. When you stopped being Moving, where were you?"

"Right here. I told you."

"But I couldn't feel you, and you didn't answer my thoughts. You were gone!"

"Oh, no, I was right here beside you as part of Air. You know that, Twig. I just stopped moving, stopped being a 'Moving Part' of Air, that's all."

"But now you are here."

"Yes, but not as I was before I stopped. I am a Moving all right, but of different Air."

"What?" Poor little Twig couldn't understand at all.

"Yes, I can be a stream of Air here or somewhere else, high Up, or low Down. If I am easy or just a little frisky I am Breeze, and when I feel brisk and steady I am Wind, but any time I am Moving, of course I am '*Moving*'. Got it, Twig?"

Twig was overwhelmed by all this, but he nodded as Moving nudged him in the side. There was so much he didn't know yet.

"And," went on Moving, "remember, Air is always here and everywhere, you know.   Just like Down, it is always here and everywhere. Down and Up are *different* from each other but both are good. Some say Down is the same as Helper. Maybe so. I don't bother about that."

Twig could hardly wait to ask Branch about Down and Helper.

"Oh, yes," Branch assured him. "Down is good. It receives our Leaves when they have finished their time with me and the other Branches. They go Down, and Dear Earth lets them rest. Down is called Helper, too, because it helps creatures without roots to stay firm on Dear Earth."

"Creatures without roots? What is *Roots*?" asked Twig.

Branch sighed as Moving brushed past him. "Let's keep that subject till later, shall we?"

6.   ROOTS AND ROOTLESS CREATURES

"Roots? Creatures without Roots?" Twig found himself thinking, wondering,

"You know about Roots," he accused Branch. "Tell me. Please," he added.

"I mostly know about our Root, and only through Big Branch at that. I learn about the creatures without Roots from Moving. Moving gets to travel even more freely than creatures without Roots do, so Moving has learned many things. However, I know about our Root from the flavors and foods that it sends Up to us. Haven't you tasted them, felt their Life Energy, Twig? Of course you have. You are part of us."

"What do you mean, Branch, 'part of us'?"

"We are all parts of Tree, silly. Don't you know that yet?"

"But - but - Tree is so - - Tree is such a great - - I mean, I'd like to see and feel Tree, and - -"

"Now listen, little Twig," Branch swayed a bit - was it irritation or was it laughter? "Listen, and taste the flavors of the sap I am sending to you..." Branch waited a moment.

"What do you taste, what do you think of?"

"Well, it is full of good juice, water and flavors and good things from - from - -"

"Yes? Water and good things are from Dear Earth, aren't they. How do they get Up to us?"

Twig couldn't answer. Why didn't Branch simply tell him?

The thought reached Branch, naturally, as all of Twig's thoughts always did. Gently now Branch replied, "You see, Tree is a great Being, just as you know even not having seen or felt Tree. And Root is the *Down* part of Tree, while the rest of us - all of us Branches and Twigs, big and little, and Buds, too - are all *Up* parts of Tree."

"Root," he went on reverently, "is the Source of all our water, Twig, except for the few Raindrops that may find us at times. Root is our Searcher, who seeks the Water that is in Dear Earth and also sends out fluids to dissolve the good things of Dear Earth, minerals and other nourishing things, and sucks them into itself, to send Up to all of us Branches and Twigs and Leaves. Besides, it is Root that fixes us solidly in Dear Earth. We Trees -" and here Branch sounded quite proud and superior, "*we* have Roots; even little grasses and things have Roots. *Some* creatures don't."

And Branch straightened rather haughtily at the thought of Rootless creatures.

Twig tried to imagine being Rootless, but when he couldn't even imagine one Root, how could he imagine No Roots?

"Then the creatures without Roots, do they flop around every time Moving comes?"

"No, they have sort of Root-like things called Legs, with a flattish flap on the end, and they Move with those. They call it *Walk*."

"Do they pull them Up out of Dear Earth to Walk?" Twig was confused.

"No, the Legs aren't Down in Dear Earth at all. The flaps on the ends sit on top of Dear Earth, and when they Walk, they pull up one Leg and its flap and move it, and then Helper pulls it Down again to Dear Earth. Then they

15

do the same for the other Leg. It is complicated...."

"Doesn't Moving help them?"

"No, Moving has nothing to do with Walk. The creature, let's say a People Larva, a Child, wants to Walk. When the Larva does it fast, it is called *Run*. They do it lots of the time."

"Why?" Twig was puzzled.

"I don't have any idea. Their thoughts are often in a turmoil. I can't get them straight. One Larva was throwing a ball - -"

"What is *Ball*?"

"That is a round thing - -"

"Does Ball have Roots?"

"Heavens no, Twig." But Branch was gentle this time. As he said once to Moving, "As I grow older, my bark gets harder and my center tougher, but my Spirit grows more patient."

"No, Twig, Ball is a *Thing*, not a *Living Thing*. Creatures play with Balls, like a game. Well, this time the Ball went Up and got stuck between two Bigger Branches. The Larva went away and came back dragging a thing that was like two Big Branches with some smaller Branches across them. The Larva leaned that thing against Tree and made its Legs go climbing Up to where the Ball was stuck and got it. Then the Larva went Down again. It was all very - -"

But this was too much for poor Twig to grasp. "Legs - Roots - Walk - Run - Ball -"

Branch perceived Twig's helpless confusion and sent a flavor of quiet understanding to him. "How is your Terminal Bud growing?" he asked, to change the subject.

7. MOVING IS FREE

One day when Moving was there Twig sent again the question: "Why are you sometimes quiet and gentle and other times quick and harsh?"

Moving gave a little swirl of laughter that made Twig rock back and forth.

"Because sometimes I am quiet and sometimes I'm not, silly," it sent the thought.

Then it added softly, "Excuse me for calling you 'silly,' Twig. You couldn't possibly know because you are stuck fast to Branch at your Union Place and can't go anywhere else. I sometimes forget that and try to get you loose to adventure to other places, as I do."

"Where is your Union Place, Moving?" asked Twig, puzzled by these remarks.

"Oh, I don't have any Union Place. As I told you, I am Free - free to go Up, or Down, or Anywhere. Sometimes I am a piece of Air here, sometimes a different piece of Air, but all Moving. That is," came its whisper with another laughing twirl, "if I am *moving*, I am *Moving*, see?'

"Then you don't have a Bigger Moving that tells you where to go, and things?"

"Well, the larger pushes and pulls of Air tell me where to go."

"Then Air is for you as Branch is to me?" Twig felt he had figured it out.

"Oh, no, not exactly like that."

"Is there anyone or anything that is for you as Tree is for me? Something that is great and powerful and everlasting and caring and..." Twig ran out of thoughts about Tree. Tree was so great and mysterious, the very Source of life.

"Well - yes, I guess Down is like that for me." Moving wafted the thought with a soft motion.

"*Down*?!" Twig was incredulous and more bewildered than ever.

"Well, make that Dear Earth instead," amended Moving. "You understand, Twig, that Dear Earth has an attraction for me, maybe a Caring, as you called it, and I do for her. She holds us close to her although she lets us be free while she does. She holds us through Helper, you know. Helper is her 'Helping Hand', as People would say. Helper can hold anything or anyone all the time, even Air, which is the freest of all. And as Helper holds us, Dear Earth draws us Down. Dear Earth is mysterious and great, and keeps all of us

17

safe and snug... I guess Dear Earth is my Union Place, all over and all around..." Moving suddenly laughed with a happy whirl, "Union Places everywhere!"

Twig had much to think about after each conversation with Moving, who seemed to Twig to be the wisest of all his acquaintances, wiser even than Branch.

Yet sometimes Twig felt a twinge of doubt. Why was it that Moving sometimes became so strong, even fearsome, when he lashed and twisted all the Branches and Twigs and tore at their Leaves as if to wrest them from their Union Places? He didn't understand. All he could do at such times was what Branch had impressed upon him, "*Just cling fast to your Union Place and do nothing else at all.*"

Moving had sent thoughts about Caring, but when Moving became terrible he didn't seem to have any Caring for anything. What about that?

And then about Helper. Twig didn't understand that, either. How could Helper be aware of everything everywhere that needed Help? And why did Helper always draw Down, not Up? Twig was told by all his acquaintances that Dear Earth was Down. How were they different?

When he asked Branch about this, Branch sent a slow steady stream of reassurance into Twig's veins: "You will understand better when your Leaves come to the time of their Leaving. They will Leave their Union Places and Helper will draw them Down... Down to Dear Earth."

8.   THE BRIGHT DIRECTION, THE BIG LIGHT, AND COLORS

Such thoughts did not really worry Twig. He had been cherishing his Leaves, taking pride in seeing how they had grown firm and well expanded with the fluids he kept sending each of them steadily, nourishing them as they formed tiny embryonic new Buds at the bases of their stems.

Now his Leaves were fully grown, eagerly soaking up the energies that came to them from the Bright Direction, rejecting only one kind of these energies. That kind they reflected back into Air. It just seemed natural.

Branch, too, felt the energies as he received the good xylem fluids sent up from Root and Bigger Branches, and then received from all his Twigs, their rich phloem fluids in return, now filled with delicate, nourishing things that the joyous Leaves had made.

Twig was slowly expanding. His length and thickness were increasing a little all the time, especially during the Bright Times.

'The Bright is called Light, you say?" he questioned Branch.

"Yes, usually. There are some other things that are Light, but mostly Light is from the Bright Direction, which is usually over *There*, on to *Up There*, and then over *There*." He indicated by sending clear thoughts to Twig as to the directions he meant.

"You mean the Bright Direction is like Moving? It Moves?" queried Twig.

"Oh, no, not like Moving at all. It is - well, it has its Pathway, *There*, to *Up There*, to *Over There*. And it sends Warmth to us, usually. Sometimes not."

"But if it Moves, then surely it IS like Moving," insisted Twig stubbornly. "Sometimes Moving is Warm, too. I can feel the Warm." For Twig, to *feel* it was to know it was *real*.

"Little Twig, take my knowledge for yourself. The Bright Direction is toward a big *Bright Spot* Up There, so Air tells me, and Moving says so, too. We have to believe them, even if we *can 't see* what they say they see. Do you understand?"

Twig nodded slowly, as Moving brushed him with a nudge indicating Moving's agreement.

"And even if our Leaves reject some of the energies that the big Light sends us as Warmth, they soak up all the rest of the energies of that sort to help them make those wonderful nourishing things that help us - all of us, and Tree-as-a-whole - to grow and be strong."

"Yes, my Leaves love all those vibrations. You say they are from the Bright Direction? But even when I can't feel any Bright Direction, I can feel the energies a little bit."

Branch rustled his twigs as Moving jostled him. "Oh, that is when the Light is obstructed from this part of Air that is here with us. They say it is still Up There or Over There somewhere, always - except during the Dark Times. In the Dark Times the Leaves and Plants can rest from making food-fluids."

Twig considered all this thoughtfully.

His Leaves felt happy, joyful. They spread out to catch all the warmth and energy they could, cooperating with each other as they worked so that each one could catch all the rays possible from the Direction of Lightness, not shadowing one another if that could be avoided.

"Why don't you like that other vibration, that one sort of energy?" Twig asked them.

"Oh, we don't need it. It doesn't suit our work right now. Branch says maybe later."

"Branch told you? Why didn't he tell me?"

"Well, you didn't ask him. Why should he tell you what is not important to you?"

"Well I ask now: Branch, why do my Leaves reject this one kind of energy'?"

"Not time yet for Leaves to want it. Later, when it is time to go Down to Dear Earth, most Leaves will soak it up. That is the time of Changing. It is natural. It is all right for them to choose which 'colors' they want."

"What are 'colors'?"

"Well, each color is 'seen' by creatures with 'vision,' when the energy from Light comes in a certain way - that is, when it comes like little vibrations of a certain speed - or - well, faster or slower, or - - "

Branch was floundering, trying to express what he himself had never 'seen', only felt.

"Funny thing," he finally ended, "Air tells me that Human creatures call Leaves and other things by the name of the energy that they *reject*! Isn't that funny? They say Leaves are *green*, and plants are *green*. And then when they do like it and want it, they change their 'color' and then Human Creatures say they are *not green*. Very odd creatures, those People, those Human Ones."

Branch shrugged as Moving shrugged against him, and Twig agreed. Human Creatures are very funny creatures.

9.   HELPER IS EVERYWHERE

Twig still wondered about "later" when his Leaves would "change color" and go Down. Right now everything seemed to be so calm and peaceful, so pleasant and just-right. He was firmly attached to Branch, surrounded by Air, and brushed softly by Moving every now and then. Light energy from the Bright Direction warmed him on that side. He felt exactly right.

So why was he wondering about a time when things might be different? It was because Branch, wise from all the things Branch had experienced, had mentioned that "later" things would Change. Twig tried to remember what his first Season had been like, so long ago....

And what about Down? He had heard Down mentioned a good many times. Even his Leaves nodded that Down drew them mildly from their floating positions when they rested.

And what about Helper? Somehow Helper and Down were often linked together in the thoughts of his friends. Was Down like a helper to Helper? Sometimes it even seemed that his Leaves meant Helper instead of Down when they rested in Moveless Air.

Root, he remembered, was always Down and loved the safety and quietness, with all the nourishing things in Down that its Rootlets could dissolve and absorb. So Down must be good.

Yet Twig also recalled the quiet mood with which Branch spoke of "later," when Leaves would change color, loosen their hold on the Twigs, and float Down.

"Even then they are held and drawn by Helper, and when the Leaves are clear Down to Dear Earth, it is Helper that assists them to nestle against her. Helper has everyone and everything safe in its influence. No one and nothing can get away. All, everyone, is safe."

A harsh voice spoke, a Crow cawing an objection. "Ha! Not always safe! Have you forgotten how one of my precious nestlings got out of the nest and lost her balance, and that terrible Helper pulled her Down? And a cat came leaping and seized my darling and ate her! If only that terrible Helper had let her alone till she got back into the nest!"

Branch, Air, and Moving were all silent. It seemed that they already knew about such things. Twig drew his thoughts into himself. It seemed from all the vibrations reaching him that this was indeed a common event.

"Well," Air sent the thought to all the others, "it is true that Helper is everywhere and has everything in its holding. That means that when someone does not keep a firmness beneath her, Helper draws that one Down very suddenly or very hard."

"She was too young to know!" cried the Crow. "Helper is old, ancient! Helper ought to know and be more careful of the young!"

"Helper is not a Who, dear Crow," Air sent the message gently. "Helper is an Allness, like Light, and like Rain, and like the Big Darkness after each Day. They are not Who, they just *Are*, equally to everyone. They do not try to help and neither do they try to hinder or hurt."

21

"Then why call this one '*Helper*'?" cried Crow.

Air sighed softly, sympathetically, "Because, dear grieving one, if it were not for Helper not even I could remain here, close to Dear Earth. Helper is related to Dear earth; they work together somehow. And Down is the way in which Helper works. Truly there is no wish in Helper to cause injury or grief. Those only occur when a certain Rule is not followed: the Rule that everything, everywhere, is held in the embrace of Helper, which draws everything Down toward Dear Earth. We must keep in mind that rule, or suffer from our carelessness or ignorance, as your nestling did. But Helper itself seems to be only part of Something Greater, I think..."

Air paused, Moveless a moment.

"What could be greater?" someone sent the query.

"Well," Air gave a sudden little swirl of conviction, "One might ask, what about the Life of your nestling? I mean the *energies of Life* in its body and its mind, and in the memories of the mother Crow, these are not in the Domain of Helper. Helper does not draw these Down. These are free - they are not held close to Dear Earth like things with shape and body.

"Helper does assist with the changes of bodies - it receives the bodies in death so that nothing and no one dies alone, ever. A dying one is always attended by Helper as its body is snuggled Down closer to Dear Earth. But its *Life-energies* - the energies of warmth and breathing and thinking - those are saved. And, I think surely there must be Something Greater than Helper to receive the Life forces... Yes, it is another Domain... here and also Somewhere Else..."

10. THE RAGING OF STORM

"*Allness* - Helper is an Allness," thought Twig, trying to figure out what that meant. He was aware of Moving brushing against him, then pushing him more vigorously, as if trying to attract his attention.

'What?" he directed the thought at Moving, who just pushed more sharply than before.

"Well, what is it?" he repeated the inquiry.

"I'm restless. Something is Changing. Something is *different*, I feel - excited! Wild!" Moving swirled and started off in a different direction, tossing up dust and things as he went. In a few moments be came back, stronger than ever, not as a Moving but as a Rushing.

Other Rushings came as well, along with a darkening of the Bright Direction and a chill in Air.

Air seemed to be in a turmoil. The Rushings became more violent, charging against Twig forcefully, twisting him, lashing him against his neighboring Twigs, tearing at his Leaves.

Twig was worried. This must be the beginning of a Bigger Storm, he realized, and he tried to recall what former Storms had been like. All he could remember was - -

But then he felt an urgent message from Branch, just as another sharp push from Rushing hit him: "*Hold - tight! Just – hold - tight!*" And he concentrated totally on his Union Place!

It was good that he did, for just then something huge struck him and might have torn him completely away from Branch if he had not held tight. "*What was that?*" he quavered to Branch.

"Nothing that matters - just one of my old Branches that had already let me withdraw its Life-energy," answered Branch. "It was time for it to go Down. Storm helped it."

"Helped it? Is Storm a Helper, too?"

"Oh, in certain ways, yes, to loosen old shapes and blow away old forms so that Helper can find better use for them somewhere and their places can be taken by newer forms."

Twig could hardly take in the meaning of Branch's thoughts, so completely occupied were his own energies now with simply holding on: "*Must – hold - tight!*"

Suddenly there was a brilliant flash, a simultaneous CRACK of noise, and a trembling in Dear Earth.   There was also a sharp click from the Tree-mind of a Tree not far away, a sound not so much of fear or pain as of mental tearing, a blast of violence. Twig felt that blast as a numbing blow to his own thoughts, too abrupt for pain or fear.

"*Lightning!*" came the thought from Branch. "Probably poor Pine-Tree got it. She grew too tall! I wondered if she'd get it sometime!"

"Too tall? Did that make her 'get it', whatever that is?" shivered Twig.

In short bursts of thought during brief moments of relative quiet, Branch told him, "Lightning often hits the tallest, the highest Up, for some reason. Always suddenly! You never know where Lightning will go, and it hits so fast that you never know it till later - so fast there is nothing but a click of your Tree-mind and you are just stunned - no feeling, no thinking, for quite a while." Branch's thoughts were sad. "It's *after* the time of numbness that you can begin to come to life again with the help of Big Tree-mind. Big Tree-mind tells your Tree what needs to be repaired, so your Tree-mind goes to work at that."

"What has to be repaired?" asked Twig, beginning to recover a little from his own shock. There was a lull in the Storm during which Branch was able to answer Twig's questions.

"Probably a long streak down her Trunk where the bark was burned away. She will cover that with new tender bark growing in from the sides. It will take a long Time, but it can be done neatly. Pine-Tree has to keep on taking care of each of her Branches and Buds, of course. Healing the wound is extra for her, but she'll get it done. Big Tree-mind has lots of experience from all the individual Tree-minds to go by, as it supervises the healing. So Pine Tree has not only her own Tree-mind but Big Pine-Tree-mind helping her."

"Will the hurt place ever stop hurting?"

"Yes, in Time it will. Oh, maybe it will ache now and then, but Pine Tree is still strong."

"Won't she be scared in Storms from now on? Scared Lightning might 'get' her again?"

"Oh, no, nothing to be scared about. Lightning hits wherever it hits, no one knows where."

"Did Lightning ever 'get' our Tree?" Twig asked.

"Once Lightning hit a Big Branch up high on our Tree. That Branch was badly hurt and its Life Forces had to be drawn back into Tree, so the Branch died. I think that was the dead one that Storm broke off and brought Down just now. It's all right. It was just a useless stick."

Again Storm raged and howled, roared and churned. Something softish struck Twig so that he bent from the blow, interrupting the fall of the object momentarily. "What was that?"

This time Branch replied with a sigh, "One of our Crows..."

Twig had not much knowledge of any birds but tiny songsters, but he knew that Crow was a bird. So Storm did harsh things to birds and to Trees. *Why* did Moving become part of such a terrible Storm? Moving was usually friendly. Helper, too, was usually really helpful.

It was bewildering; he didn't understand at all; but for now he *just held on tight* - and let Storm's wild winds and slashing rain-drops rage.

11. LEARNING, WORKING, MATURING

Storm gradually diminished, leaving Twig both relieved and exhilarated. Air, likewise, seemed to be both refreshed and relieved. Storm had been a great event, frightening but exciting. After it quieted into a gentle rain, Twig and Air and Branch and all other beings felt rejuvenated.

The days became a series of quiet Changes, the Bright Direction each Day moving from Over There to Up Above, and then to over That Way, and then followed by the Big Dark and coolness.

Twig was accustomed to these Changes and now focused his attention on certain spots along his length, on the end of Terminal Sprout especially. These places felt different - eager, somehow, and he felt that he wanted to help them get - - what?

Those places wanted to get bigger, stronger, with more definite shapes inside of them. They wanted to grow and become. Become? Yes, become something... in the future?

Oh, yes, they were his new Buds! He had felt these starting when his Leaves were fully grown. Each Leaf had a tiny Bud-spot developing at the base of its stem, at its Union Place.

Joyously he kept pouring the nourishing sap from Branch to each of the tiny new Buds as well as to his Leaves, sending each one as much as it could use. As long as Root sent up fluids to Branch, Twig had plenty to send to each.

His Leaves had become fully mature, fluttering or swinging as Moving pushed them playfully, the tiny new bud-spots at the base of their stems hardly noticeable. Each Leaf accepted the presence of its new Bud-spot, sharing the sap from Twig with it matter-of-factly, knowing it as a new family member.

Branch was calm and happy these summer days, both during the Bright Times and the Dark Times. Twig therefore felt safe and happy, too.

Sometimes he received faint memories from Branch of other times that had not been happy - times of dryness, for instance, when Root could find little Water to send up. Tree had suffered in all its Branches and had been able to form only small Leaves. In fact - as Branch recalled sadly - Tree had been forced to make hard decisions to cut off fluids entirely from certain Twigs and Branches and pull back their Life forces, in order to keep the rest alive. (This awareness was stored back in Twig's large Tree-memory as an inert knowledge not needed now.) Those branches had accepted quietly that they needed to let their Life-forces withdraw. Where did the Life-forces go? They didn't go Down, that was certain.

Other knowledge was there, too, more clear and immediate, such as the work of Leaves. Ah, his Leaves. They kept busily soaking up the warm energies that bathed them each moment that the Bright Direction sent its light. Even when the Bright Direction was obscured by Clouds, Twig and the Leaves could feel the energies coming, the energies of yellow and red that they used in making food substances to pour into the sap for Tree.

Air had told him that the light-energies could bounce from one thing, like a Leaf, to another thing like another Leaf or a Branch, or even the Eyes of other creatures like People.

He tried to explain Eyes to Twig. Twig got the idea that Eyes were something like Bud-places.

People with Eyes called Leaves "Green." That was funny, because that was the Color the Leaves didn't keep. Not in these Days of summer, anyway.

12. CHANGING, CHANGING COLOR, PREPARING TO GO DOWN

Twig became aware that the days were slowly becoming less warm. The Bright Direction was changing its position gradually day by day and the Dark times were almost chilly. Now somehow his Leaves felt that they wanted that Green energy. They eagerly absorbed it and began to turn away the other energies that used to be so welcome. They were Changing! They were changing work habits, and therefore changing color.

It seemed that many things were Changing, gradually, quietly, inevitably. Even Dear Earth seemed to be preparing for a Change. Twig and his Leaves were preparing for a Resting, all except the new Buds. They were surrounding themselves with a tough sheath of waxy scales, preparing less for Resting than for protection against - What?

Twig sought in his memory for what had taken place when he was just a Twiglet. He tried to recall also what Branch and Air had told him. Yes, that the Big Cold would be coming before long, and it was time now to Prepare.

When all was properly Prepared, then Twig and the Buds would be safe while they rested during the Big Cold. Even during the Cold, however, Twig felt that he and the other Twigs, like Tree and all its Branches, would be very quietly increasing in girth; and all the new Buds on all the Twigs would be slowly growing in inner complexity as they increased in size.

The Buds were the brave parts of Tree that were to prepare silently all during the Cold and unfold first, as the Big Cold eventually diminished...

For now, the time for work was over. The Leaves swung easily as Moving teased them to play with Light and Rain, and they happily bounced away the energies of yellow and orange into Air. They felt different, they felt they could be on a holiday! No work to do! Just swing in the breezes and enjoy the time! They also felt that soon they might let go of Twig. Their Union Places? They hardly thought of those now.

Twig felt that the Union Places of his Leaves with him were being crowded by the new Buds. Well, it seemed to be all right, somehow, even when the Union Place of one Leaf was almost shut off.

"What about you?" Twig sent the question to the Leaf.

"I think - that maybe I am feeling toward Down more than usual," Leaf replied hesitantly. It was the first time in Leaf's life that this had happened. It was a new experience. "It isn't scary, but it is - *different.*"

Moving came along at that moment, swung Leaf to and fro and asked, "Are you ready?"

"Ready for what?"

"Oh, you know for the Big Ride, the Big Fall, The Down-Going," chuckled Moving.

Twig didn't feel it was a matter for laughing. He wondered how Leaf felt. Leaf, however, seemed to accept the question seriously. He answered Moving just as seriously.

"It seems to be all right, even if it is *different.* I guess I am ready. How do I know?"

As Leaf sent that thought, "I am ready," his stem bent at the narrowed Union Place where the new bud was growing and suddenly the stem parted from Twig, and Leaf was free!

At first Leaf felt the gentle support of Air as always, softly drawing him Down, and he felt the quiet push of Moving, but this time there was a new, strange feeling. It was exciting, beautiful, a little disturbing... but if felt all right, even if *different.*

"I have never done this before! It - it is free - it is - well, I still feel the Down, so I guess Helper is with me, as it promised, and Dear Earth is waiting for me. Give me a few twirls as I go, before I am Down, Moving!"

And Moving obliged with a happy little whirl-wind, sending Leaf circling colorfully, joyously, before he settled Down and relaxed, nestled softly against Dear Earth.

Twig was aware of the sudden absence of Leaf from his Union Place, but Twig also had to think of his other Leaves, who also were loosening their attachments. Twig recalled more clearly how it had been long ago, when he had been a tiny Twiglet with a Leaf or two. It was hard to remember whether he had felt afraid - no, not that - maybe more a surprised feeling, when he had become aware that his first Leaf was leaving him.

"The first time for anything is a surprise," he thought now, "and the second time is rather a surprise, but not as much. One can think back the second time to what came afterward."

With this attitude of quiet expectancy, Twig felt the departure of his other Leaves one by one, as he aided the silent increase in strength of the tiny buds remaining. He firmed their Union Places and sent them his own life-fluids. They must be kept safely part of him all through the Storms and freezing times of the Big Cold.

Branch was similarly occupied with Preparations, continuing to send good sap - but more slowly now - to all its Twigs to assist in their Preparations, as Tree was sending sap to each Big Branch and smaller Branches. Root and Trunk were keeping some of the nourishment for themselves, continuing to grow quietly in girth and toughness. The outer layer, the bark, of Trunk and of each Branch became a little thicker as the cooling days grew colder.

One morning when the Light from the Bright Direction brought very little warmth, Twig felt Moving whip him against another Twig. The contact made a rattling noise, a vibration of chilly dryness without the soft rustling vibrations of his Leaves. He felt almost brittle.

"Well, I'll just hold tight, and let Branch worry about things," he decided. If I lived through that other Big Cold, I'll get through this one, too."

And, not realizing what a philosopher he had become, he let his thoughts float passively... until... he began to sense some other thoughts... bigger ones than his... Whose?

As Twig allowed his own thoughts to remain silent, those larger thoughts became more clear. It seemed that Twig had somehow tuned into the thoughts of *Tree*.

Tree was sensing all the parts of himself at once, not in confusion, as it would have seemed to little Twig, but as a clean, firm Tree-as-a-whole: Root, Branches, Twigs, Buds, and even some of the Leaves that strewed the ground of Dear Earth. Tree-mind was focusing on all his various parts at once, sending his awareness into them, testing them for any needs each might be having. It seemed that Tree-mind was always doing this. Now he was Preparing for Change.

The thoughts of Tree-mind were large ones, encompassing his entire body and also the parts of Dear Earth around his Roots and the portions of Air among his Branches.

As Twig found himself in contact with these great Thoughts he felt himself very small indeed and yet immensely large - as huge as Tree himself. He remembered that once he had wanted to see and talk to Tree... and now he *realized for the first time* what he had been told but could not understand: that he *really was a part of Tree*. He, little Twig, was a true part of great Tree! The knowledge, the sudden understanding was both incredible and glorious.

He remembered the lifeless body of the Branch that Storm had broken off and cast Down. His own Branch had seemed quite matter-of-fact about it all. In fact, the sadness of Branch had mostly been that Tree had to let all his Branches become so thirsty that season; that he had to let some Branches wither in order that other Branches might live.

Trying to figure this out brought Twig back into his own familiar small thoughts again. Branch seemed to know this and sent his own thoughts.

"Yes, Twig, sometimes we have living bodies, and sometimes we let them go Down to Dear Earth. And sometimes we help others and sometimes others help us, and it all works together somehow. Don't worry. It is all right. Ask Air. Ask Dear Earth. They will tell you better than I can."

These ideas didn't clear up Twig's confusion but they did bring him some comfort.

"All right, I'll ask Air and Dear Earth sometime," he resolved sleepily. He had always felt that Tree must be almost his entire universe. After this momentary enlargement of his thoughts, however, he realized that Air and Dear Earth were both greater even than Tree. How enormous was the Universe!

13. OTHER TREES, DIFFERENT TREES

A few more days went by. Warmth and light alternated with nights of darkness, when the Bright Direction was absent and Air became cold. Moving came and went as usual, but sometimes seemed to be absent.

Twig called to him during one of those times, and Moving stirred, "You and all your questions! Can't you let a Moving be Moveless *for even one minute?*"

"What's a *minute?*" asked Twig.

There was a quick sigh, almost of irritability. "Oh, all right, what's the next question?"

"The next question? Well, I often feel a tap, and I guess it is from a Leaf that has let go of its Union Place and has fallen against me as it floats Down. Is that it? And if it is, then there must be lots of Leaves still letting go now. Is that so?"

Moving stirred again, sluggishly. "Yes, that's it. That's the way things are going now."

"Why?"

"Why? Oh, for twiggish sakes, Twig! Haven't you heard? This is the *time* for Leaves to let go and be helped Down to Dear Earth by Helper. You should know all that! Your own Leaves did!"

Twig refused to let his thoughts be stopped. "Well, but now the noise you make when you blow through Tree has changed, Moving. You used to make a different sound."

"Oh, that," said Moving. "That's because there were many Leaves on your Tree that liked to flutter when I went through them. They'd swing against each other and make little clapping sounds."

"Yes, that's what I mean. Those noises made me feel happy and nice."

"Yes, I suppose so... and now there are fewer of them, so they don't make as much of the tapping noise as the many Leaves did in Sumner. So now they sound different."

"Yes, but sometimes there is another sound, *different*, like a whispering or sighing, not like a clapping or tapping. Do you make that, too, Moving?"

Moving stretched and joggled Twig. He was gradually waking up and was ready to tease Twig. Or even to teach him something new.

"Oh, that. That must be when I move through the Needles of the Evergreen Trees."

"What's *Needles*?"

"Those are the Leaves of the Evergreen Trees. They are narrow, like the stems of your Leaves. They don't have the wide parts that flutter and clap each other."

Twig tried hard to imagine it. "Like stems? No wide parts? Then how do they take in the Light Energies and make food? They are useless!"

Moving jostled Twig. "Well, youngster, you have learned something about your own Leaves and the others of your own Tree, haven't you!"

Then he took pity on Twig and explained, "See, little one, the Evergreen Trees are called so because their Leaves stay what is called 'green' all through the Big Cold. They don't let go in the Getting-colder time, as the Leaves of your Tree do. And when I move through the Needles, for me it is like going through a strainer, a sieve (as People would say), and the sound they make is more like a whisper, not like clapping. I call it 'sighing.' They sigh when I move through. And they do make food."

Twig's next question was ready: "They make food all through the Big Cold? Don't they get tired and want to let go and drift Down? And let Helper snuggle them close to Dear Earth?"

"Oh, the oldest needles do let go and they let me push them free so they can go Down."

"Are there any Twigs on Evergreen Trees?"

"Oh, yes, lots of Twigs. And each Twig has lots of Needles."

Twig felt relieved. There was at least one thing about these Evergreen Trees that he could understand. He felt a sort of comradeship now with these strange Evergreen Trees.

Moving anticipated the next question. "There are lots of Evergreen Trees, Twig, not only here, near your own Tree, but in many, many other places - - many, many, many other Evergreen Trees. And there are many other *deciduous* Trees like your own, that drop their Leaves in the fall - - many, many, many other Trees similar to your own Tree. I see them every day. *Many of them, and many different kinds!*"

Twig's imagination was strained beyond his capacity. He hung silent. The universe was so much bigger than he could imagine. The universe must be as big as Air, as big as Dear Earth!

All of a sudden his feeling of being lost in an immensity became changed into a deep feeling that, in all the Immensity, somehow he was held safe, secure, by a tremendous vastness larger than all the Trees, as if Dear Earth

31

herself held him within her somehow, as if Helper kept him safe within the great tender grasp of Dear Earth. He didn't understand it, but he nestled softly against his Union Place with dear, reliable Branch, and let himself drift off to sleep in this great Safety.

14. THE GREAT COMING DOWN

One day during the Big Cold Twig felt a sudden bad-feeling urge - to get away from - from - something threatening, he didn't know what. How could a Twig get away from anything? But he knew this was something very bad. He focused to Branch, and to his horror found that Branch felt the same way, an acute fear of something terrible that seemed about to happen.

"What is it?" This time Twig's question was timid.

Branch sent back a similar quaver of fear. "Those People standing there underneath Tree, they are sending thoughts about doing something to Tree - our Tree - and it is bad. The thoughts are about destroying Tree - or parts of Tree. Oh, why are they sending thoughts of things like that? The noises from their face-parts, their Talking, are saying the same thoughts. I'm afraid!"

Twig became even more frightened at Branch's admission of fear. He wanted to shrink away, do something to get away from those feelings. Instead he just tried to shrink up closer to Branch at his Union Place and held tight. What else could a Twig do?

Gradually he felt Branch sending on to him the flavors Branch was receiving from Big Branch and Tree-as-a-whole: "Well, if that is what is to occur, that is what will happen. We are forewarned, so let us Prepare for such a change. We will be firm, brave, true to our nature."

Somehow that courage was sent through all the parts of Tree, clear into the Twigs, and Twig responded, still holding tight to his Union Place with Branch. He felt stronger, more calm.

Not long after the terrifying thoughts had struck Tree the People went away and came back in a big Car they called Truck. The People unloaded some things and began to work. Their machines made loud noises and heavy vibrations.

The terrible vibrations came up through all the Branches, and Tree trembled. The sound-vibrations, too, sawed through Air and screeched against all the Twigs and on out into Air in all directions.

Twig clung steadfastly to his Union Place and *just held tight*. He didn't know what has happening, but he did know that in all the events that he didn't understand, he must *always just hold tight*. Branch and Tree would take care of things with Air and Dear Earth.

So although this new experience was scary, Twig wasn't really concerned until he felt Branch begin to sway and creak.

"What is it?" His thought quavered out into Air.

"People are sawing off some Big Branches of your Tree," came the quiet answer. Air did not seem to be greatly disturbed by this horrendous idea. Twig could not understand.

"Why do they do that?"

"Who knows? People are strange creatures. They do many things not understandable."

"What will happen?" Now Twig was really worried.

"Oh, the Branches sawed off will go Down."

"What then? Will I go Down, too?"

"Oh, yes. Eventually Helper helps all things go Down anyway." Air was still calm.

"What will happen then?" Twig sent out the question with urgency.

"Little Twig, be at ease. Just let things happen. People are powerful; they do whatever they feel like doing, for any reason they feel like having. We can not prevent them. So we must simply let things occur, and afterward do whatever we can to repair the damages and start again."

"We can repair the damages?" That sounded more hopeful to Twig.

"Well, within limits, of course. In any case, we can only go along with events as they occur. I advise you to *just hold tight* to your Branch and not let anything else bother you."

Twig, still trembling from those terrible vibrations, tried to follow this advice, but it was hard to ignore them and the horrible sound-vibrations that kept swarming around him. He concentrated on simply holding tight to Branch.

And then Branch began to droop Down faster... and faster...

There were some awful sensations of rending and tearing transmitted to Twig through Branch. Then a feeling as of swooping Down, seized by Helper to strike Dear Earth in a tremendous CRASH! and Twig felt himself being lashed back and forth, whipped this way and that for several moments - which yet seemed like a very long time. It made him feel disoriented. He closed his mind tight and just held on.

The feelings and thoughts from Branch seemed to be disoriented, too. Even the thoughts from Tree were disturbed and uncertain. Surely Tree would know what this was all about! The only thoughts from Tree that Twig could make out were something like, *"Just so - Root and Trunk - and Dear Earth - remain - we can manage... Severe Change... Must wait - till later - for Big Tree-Mind - to help me."*

Tree shivered another time as a second Big Branch was torn away and Helper brought it Down with a crash. Even Biggest Branch was not spared. The People's terrible noises and tools sawed and screamed until Biggest Branch was detached from Trunk and Helper brought it Down with a shattering, prolonged noise as its many Branches, in quick succession, struck Dear Earth.

Then there was a lull, as the People stood and sent thoughts and noises to one another. "There, I guess that'll take care of it," was the thought from one.

"Yeah, People shouldn't plant Trees under light wires. Trees grow up and have to be cut back."

"Yep, there are regulations about plantings. I guess these were planted before the wires were strung."

"Well, anyway, we left the Tree itself. Too bad it's so lop-sided now."

"Yeah, used to be a rather nice-looking Tree. Oh, well, we've done our work. Come on, the trash men and the chipping machines will soon be here. They'll take care of the rest."

Twig didn't understand any of this except that Tree was no longer "nice-looking." He also understood that he himself, as part of Branch, was among the portions of Tree that were no longer portions of Tree but were scattered around on Dear Earth, Down on Dear Earth...

He was still holding tight to his Union Place with Branch. Suddenly there was a different noise. Vibrations of shouting and that noise called Laughing, the sounds made by the Larvae of People when they feel happy. He felt something warm grasp Branch and begin making up-and-down movements along with the Laughing noises. Branch was curved up then down, repeatedly as the Larva jumped on him. The Twigs were all being whipped up and down, too, but were not being drawn Down in the same way as before.

"Looky, I'm a kangaroo!" shouted the Larva, making Branch bounce him higher.

"What's - a - *kangaroo*?' Twig tried to think to Branch, but his thoughts got scrambled by the motions and the noises. All he could make out of Branch's thoughts were, *"Just – have - to - wait - till - things- quiet - down - -"*

15. NO UNION PLACE, INTO A NEW DOMAIN

After a while things did seem to quiet down. The Larvae went away somewhere, still making those noises of Laughing. Then some adult People came and began to pick up the parts of Tree that were Down on Dear Earth. They sawed Biggest Branch and other Big Branches into short chunks and threw these heavy parts onto a big flat Car and began stuffing the smaller parts, like Branches and Twigs, into the end of a different Car, which made horrible noises and sent out smells of sap and Life Forces...

Twig *tried to hold tight* to his Union Place with Branch, but suddenly felt himself stripped away, his Union Place torn wide open. He felt helpless, lost. What was he without Branch? Who indeed was he? And what was Branch, whose form was now being fed into that awful Car...?

As he lay there, hurt, bereft of everything he had ever known or trusted, he felt a soft touch, as Moving wafted over and stroked him, caressing him.

"Sorry, Twig, but these things happen. Really, it's all right. You'll see. Ask Dear Earth."

"Moving! What happens now? What do I do now? Where is Branch?"

"No, ask your Questions of Air and Dear Earth now, Twig. Ask them. They know."

Twig recalled other times when he had asked Questions and had been told to ask Air or Dear Earth. It seemed that there were limits as to what his friends knew. Well, then he would turn to Dear Earth for Answers.

He did not even need to form a Question for Dear Earth herself began to send soft thoughts into his mind, thoughts something like, "Just rest for now, little Twig. For now, Rest."

Aware that sap was going to be leaving his body and that his Life Forces were draining away, Twig let his awareness nestle closer to that gentle, all-pervading thought, "For now, Rest."

He had received similar thoughts and feelings from his Leaves after they had gone Down, too, so he knew that each of them had felt this quiet trustful touch with Dear Earth, just as he felt it now. He let his awareness drift, and it seemed to be attracted to something Down below.

Without emotion, he recognized it as his own Twig-body Down there on Dear Earth. It seemed to be quite all right that it was there and that his awareness was Up here above it, even if this position was unfamiliar. He became aware of a feeling inside, as if something felt like smiling. What was there to be smiling about on this awful day?

The tender smiley feeling grew within him, a big warm feeling that made him feel safe and comforted. Then the feeling began to send thoughts into his insides, almost as Branch used to send thoughts through his sap. Could this be the way Dear Earth talked to creatures? Twig let his mind focus on what the feeling was making him think about.

"Of course, dearie," the warm feeling welled up into his mind. "This is the way we talk, now that you have become part of me. And yes, I'll be glad to answer as many of your Questions as I can." There was that feeling of smiling again, brighter now, clearer.

"You can answer all my Questions?" Twig had a long list of Questions inside his mind! "Then why did People chop and saw up Tree and treat even Trunk and Biggest Branch and all the other Branches that way? And leave Tree so lop-sided and not-beautiful?" Twig felt so sad.

"Dearie," came that warm, strong, safe feeling again, "Dearie, People are very complicated creatures. They make very complicated Plans, and some Plans they build long before other Plans. If their Plans interfere with each other, some of the Plans will be destroyed by the very People that built them. In this case they were destroying the parts of Tree that threatened their Wires strung on the tall Trunks of old Trees whose Life Forces had been withdrawn long ago."

"The Wires were not more important than Tree's Branches!"

"The Wires carry Forces that People consider very precious - not Life Forces, but others that do many important things for People. Tree's Branches did not harm the Wires in calm Air, but when Moving became strong, especially if he became Storm, he thrashed the Branches of Tree against the Wires and threatened to break them. That is why the People cut down the Branches."

"But - but - but..." Twig wanted to say much more but somehow that calm strong feeling inside of him was quieting his own small feelings and sad objections...

"There, there, dear, when you get past the Time Domain it will be much clearer. Now just see us all in the Past of Time. See how it is?" The quiet voice inside of him paused and Twig felt his awareness expanding, expanding... saw forests of trees, most of the Trees healthy but some growing old, other forests thinned by the machines and houses of People... then changing - and changing - -

He didn't understand what he saw. He felt Dear Earth's thoughts inside him again.

"Another Question, little Twig? You are seeing the Past. All of my dear children are still here in the Time-Past and Time-Future Domains, not in the Time-Present Domain where you have lived as Twig. Later you will see, dearie, but for now just see this glimpse." And Dear Earth became very still... and a Knowing came inside of Twig...

He felt his dear Leaves there close to him, he felt their vibrations, tasted their flavors, he knew them, each one! They were here, as much alive as he himself. And Branch was here, and his Union Place with Branch was intact, absolutely solid! And then he found himself a Bud again. It was all too strange, too overwhelming. Twig couldn't grasp all this.

"I just can't - - It's all so wonderful, but it can't be true - I don't understand," he said to the visions.

"No, dearie, you can't understand. Even I don't understand all of it but I do know that I keep all my children and their Pasts safe in my Memory, always, every bit, and *it is real*. People are sometimes able to contact my Memory. They have even given it a People name." There was a feeling of amusement. "They call it 'The Memory of Nature' or even 'The Akashic Records'. Well, People are my children, too, remember. Very complicated ones!" And Dear Earth's smiling became brighter inside of Twig's mind. He had to let his own feelings smile a little with Dear Earth's smiley ones.

"There now, dearie, that's better." He felt the warm thought filling him up inside. "That's just a brief glimpse, you know. Later as you become settled into us it will feel natural. Now why not just let your own feelings drift peacefully? The whole of Air is free to you now, you know."

Twig did feel as if he needed a period of just letting his thoughts drift. Even having this little peek into the new Domain had opened so wide a mental vista that he just couldn't - it was all just too - - Well, he hoped Dear Earth was right when she said it would all feel familiar later.

One thing he did know already: that Dear Earth was close, and warm,

37

and wise, and tender, and she cared about him.

He watched as Helper snuggled his cast-off body closer Down against Dear Earth, and then he let his mind drift softly alongside of Moving, as Moving drifted through the quiet Air.

16. QUESTIONS FROM TWIG, ANSWERS FROM AIR

Moving surely knew that Twig was full of questions but he said nothing. Was it simply politeness or was it that perhaps Moving didn't care very much to give Answers today? What was it he had said, "Ask your Questions of Air and Dear Earth?" Had something changed in his relationship with Twig?

"Why don't you want to - -" Twig began.

Moving ignored the thought.

"I won't ask you very many Questions, just a few now and then," offered Twig.

Moving ignored him again. Then Twig directed his Question to Air. "Why won't Moving answer my thoughts any more?"

Air, impersonal as always, sent back, "You are in another Domain now, Twig. Moving is still in the Time Domain where you used to be. He can't see or feel you now that your body has gone Down, except that he sees it Down there and can touch it when he goes by. He knows it isn't your mind Or your Life Forces. He has his own adventures now and doesn't share yours."

"But he is part of you, Air. You said so. And you are answering me."

"I am an Allness, always here and everywhere, just being myself and doing my tasks, that's all. Moving responds to directives from larger portions of me, and they respond to directives from still larger forces."

"Dear Air, there are so many things I don't understand, things that seem wrong, terrible, like what the People did to Tree! That just isn't right!"

"Those things happen, for many reasons or perhaps for no good reason at all. In a way I know the frustrated feeling you have in a small way now, Twig - for in other circumstances I feel frustrated and helpless and have a strong feeling of wrongness, too..."

Air sighed and gave part of its sense of frustration to Moving as Moving went by. Moving turned moody, almost gloomy, and poured himself Down to wallow mournfully among some weeds, so strong was the influence of that great sad sigh.

LOUISE IRELAND-FREY, M.D.

"Oh, no, not again," thought Moving.

Air explained to Twig, "I am thinking of the ways I am dirtied and polluted in other places - not here, but in many parts of Dear Earth where many People and creatures are in misery from hunger or cold. The breathings of those People and other creatures are full of pain, urgent needs, longings, envies, angers... In other places great fires blaze through the forests and send smoke and Life Forces of Trees and Birds and other Creatures up into me... And sometimes Dear Earth gives a big Belch and sends up dust, fire, ashes, chunks of herself, and foul odors - all of these filling great portions of me with pains and evil smells and darkness... And besides these, all the filthy vibrations of rage and hate from other Domains... There are many such places.

"Yes, little one, I do share your little feelings. Yet, because I am an Allness, I still just do what I have to do and can't do anything else. Not even if maybe it is a wrongness. My one task is to keep Air around Dear Earth for her creatures to breathe with, to sing with, to laugh with, to weep with... and even to receive the dirtiness and dark things put in."

Twig was silent. All this was too great for his mind to grasp. This was a common state for Twig, the "I don't understand" type of feeling. Yet he felt a greater understanding of Air, a sympathy recognizing sympathy from another. It seemed that Air did feel sadness. Twig wanted to offer comfort in some way but didn't know how. Air was so great, so mysterious, so vast.

17. QUESTIONS FROM TWIG, ANSWERS FROM DEAR EARTH

"Air says you Belch sometimes. Why is that?" was the next Question Twig asked.

Dear Earth seemed astonished.

"Belch? I *belch*? Oh, well, no doubt it seems like that to Air!" And Twig felt her chuckle inside him. "It doesn't feel like that to me. You see, Twig, my body is very large and as I grow older it begins to shrink a little, as many bodies do when aging. As it shrinks, it causes wrinkles in my skin and pressures inside me. In certain pimply places I feel itches and tingling sensations that tell me pressures are building up, heat increasing, and then Pain begins in a pimple. The Pain can be relieved if I let the pressure be released. So I let the pimple erupt and that is what Air calls a Belch. I know it

39

does pollute a large portion of Air for a while. For that I apologize, but it can't be helped. It certainly is a relief to me."

Twig was awed by all this information - things he had never thought of in his whole life. Were there other such things about Dear Earth that he had no knowledge of? He asked her.

"Well, in other places my skin has been scraped away by People. They leave great raw wounds on my mountainsides and fill the valleys with the shards and rubbish of their work, and neglect to take care of the Life Forces that they have disrupted by all this. I do wish my People children would calm down their desires and listen more respectfully to my other children's needs! But People are very complicated..."

"Why do they scrape away your skin?" was Twig's next question.

"To get some things they want from under my skin, minerals and coal and such."

"What is Coal?" Twig wanted to know.

"Coal in the Present is what used to be living Plants and other Creatures in the Past. It took a long, long Time to make that Change come about. Shall I show you, dearie, in what People call Fast Forward?"

Twig let his own small mind become passive and felt a great forest take shape in Dear Earth's Memory. It was filled with crowded Trees, Bushes, and other plants, and also with many Beasts of all sizes. Gradually the scene Changed - the forest was flattened; layer upon layer of sediments from Water and of dust from Air covered it - the weight grew immense, the Plant-forms were smashed into a hard layer which was then covered by still more layers of sediment.

"The black hard layer is what remains in the Present of what in the Past were the deep layers of Plants and Forests," explained Dear Earth. "Now People want the Coal for many uses. Sometimes they dig for it in deep holes through my skin."

"Does that make it itch?"

"Oh, dearie, let's not worry about it now. You do ask many Questions! Air warned me." The feeling inside of Twig was gentle, amused, and not at all cross.

"Thank you, Dear Earth, I do want to learn all I can from you," he sent, politely. He felt her kindly response before she withdrew her thoughts.

Twig did try to answer many Questions himself. He truly didn't want to bother Dear Earth with too many Questions, but, really, there were so many he just couldn't figure out for himself - like the problem of dust and "Belches" from Dear Earth that made Air dirty. Wasn't it Storm that churned up so much dust and trash in Air, making it dirty? That wasn't from a "Belch..." That was due to huge Movings in Air itself. Why did Air make itself dirty?

At last he decided he would have to ask someone about that. He felt a little hesitant to ask Air, so he asked Dear Earth instead. "Why does Air sometimes make big Storms that are dirty?"

Dear Earth's smile inside him was becoming familiar by now. "Dearie, Air sometimes has feelings that demand a response, feelings that are too powerful to be ignored, so Air responds in whatever way it finds easiest or most effective. Some of those ways you won't be able to understand, little one. They involve huge Movings and Rushings, great *differences* in pressures and therefore differences in the way Air feels Helper drawing it Down toward me. So the Movings and Rushings and the Differences get to swirling around each other, stirring up everything that gets in the way. People give names to the swirlings, names like Cyclone or Typhoon, Hurricane or Tornado... People fear them because they are so powerful, but they are just ways in which Air has to respond to the Changes it feels in itself.

"If they churn up dust and dirt," she went on, "then Helper afterward assists in drawing such things Down to me again and lets Air become clear and clean. That is part of Helper's task, you know."

18. HELPER IS AN ALLNESS, IS DEAR EARTH, TOO?

Twig was thinking. "Do - Are you - - Dear Earth, are you an Allness, like Air and Helper?"

This time the feeling inside him was almost a laughter. "Oh, dearie me, no! I am a Being like Tree, only larger. I am a living Being with Mind and Feelings and a part that Continues on. Yes, dearie, I used to be..."

Dear Earth paused a long time, then continued, "Well, that story goes way back to when I wasn't yet an Earth at all."

"Were you a Bud back then?" Twig couldn't help asking.

Again, that smiley feeling inside. "Oh, no, nothing like a Bud; a *Nebula*, more like a Cloud..." Dear Earth paused again, thinking back to that Cloud. Twig remained quiet, too.

Finally dear Earth began again, "When the Cloud became more dense it

41

became warmer, and became a hot ball, which slowly became cooler and got a skin over the outside. That was my first skin, dearie. I could feel that I was an individual Being and not a scattered Cloud. As I grew older, however, I began to shrink a little, as I told you, and my skin began to get wrinkled. Some of the wrinkles cracked and shoved against each other and made strong vibrations and harsh noises. The edges of some wrinkles were pushed Down and under the edges of others.

"My skin felt better after these Changes had taken place, but until the Changes had occurred my skin felt tight, felt pressures and heat and uncomfortable feelings."

"Like itches?"

Dear Earth chuckled. "Well, perhaps we might use that term, but much bigger than itches. More like the way a mother creature feels when her baby is about to be born."

Now Twig was utterly bewildered. "I - I guess I don't understand about that." He felt Dear Earth soothe him.

"No, dearie, not yet... But think, Twig: Right now, what do you feel like? Who are you right Now?"

Again Twig felt mentally lost. "Why, I am a Twi - -" he stopped. "I - I *used* to be a Twig and Now I feel bigger than a Twig... maybe like a Branch? No, not a Branch. Like a Tree? No, not yet anyway... Dear Earth, won't you help me? I just don't know these things!"

He felt Dear Earth's gentle teasing in his mind. "Run out of Knowledge into more Questions, have you, dearie?

"Well, soon I'll let you in on some more secrets. For instance, there is a Big Helper that is between me and Lesser Light that People call Moon, and Moon responds to me through Big Helper. Ease your mind for now and just enjoy." And she withdrew her presence leaving only a restful stillness.

Part of Twig's mind kept thinking about those other secrets Dear Earth would tell him. She had mentioned a Big Helper, something about the Moon. He must ask about that.

Then a terrific thought leaped into his mind: If there is a Big Helper, is there a Bigger Helper as well? The idea shocked him - This was one Questions he really, truly, absolutely must ask Dear Earth! Maybe there is even - - is even - - even a *Biggest Helper*? A *Biggest Allness*?

It seemed that his mind was kept stretching and stretching. How long ago it was that he had been just a simple little Twig, and thought that Tree was almost the whole universe!

He had felt that Tree was eternal, indestructible. But now Tree was a broken mutilated thing, terribly wounded, in deep shock, waiting until Big Tree-Mind could help him. The tragedy of this had reached Twig's own feelings even through the process of Twig's Down-going, but - still more amazing - had been relieved by the vision that Dear Earth had given him, of the living Past, in which Tree was strong and symmetrical and beautiful still - or again - or whatever - but real!

Now Twig's mind puzzled over that Question Dear Earth had asked, 'What are you Now? Who are you Now?' Well, let that wait until later.

Instead, he took the first opportunity to inquire about the Big Helper of Dear Earth.

"Yes, dearie, you know about the Moon?"

"Yes, Moving says it is a Bright Direction that is not as bright as the Day-time one. Moving says the Bright Directions are caused by Bright Spots over *there*, moving to Up *there*, and then *to over that way*. I think they are in Air, way up high. But if they move, they are Movings." Twig's last remark was sent out with a trace of stubbornness.

"Perhaps it is more complicated, dearie. Let's think instead that Moon is a Being like me but smaller, and that Moon is swinging around me as she flies. Her flying makes her feel like flying off away from me but through Big Helper I hold her to her pathway, so it seems that she courses around me in a circle."

"Through Air? She is flying through Air up high?"

"No, Air has told you already that Air only extends a certain distance out away from my skin, dearie. Beyond Air is what is called Space, where there is no Air but there are forces like Helper, and Light, and Thoughts, and many others coming and going far and near. As I said, it can seem complicated, but the main idea is that Big Helper is much stronger than my Helper down here. Moon feels Big Helper's power, and even though Moon is so much smaller than I, I feel her power as Moon pulls at the waters on my skin, the oceans and lakes, and also the rocks and forests and everything, though they may not feel or notice the pulling."

"Isn't it all quite dangerous? Why all that pulling, anyway?"

Dear Earth sent her smiling presence into Twig's mind. "Without it things would all be flying away from me, little one. Isn't that more dangerous? No, the Helpers are truly Helpers. They are Allnesses, working

THE EDUCATION OF TWIG

exactly in an impartial way, in their case, more strongly on things that are 'heavy' or 'dense,' more lightly on things that are small or feathery and light."

When Dear Earth paused, Twig began to remember that stupendous Crash when Tree's Big Branch was cut off. And Biggest Branch had certainly been heavy! Was that why it had been brought Down with such force by Helper, whereas smaller Branches had fallen more lightly?

"Yes, dearie, you are getting close. Beyond Helper's work here is the still stronger, wider work of Big Helper binding Moon and me into our planet/satellite relationship. Greater and more powerful yet is the work of Bigger Helper, holding me so that I move in a circle around Great Light - I mean around what you call Bright Spot - really a great Being far beyond Moon."

Twig took a while to try to understand all this. Finally he sent out that Question that had shocked him so deeply when he had first thought of it. "Dear Earth, is there - - is there a *Biggest Helper*?"

Dear Earth didn't seem shocked at all. She paused, then sent a quietness like reverence into Twig's mind. "Dearie, I believe so. I know for sure about Bigger Helper, which is far more powerful than Big Helper and firmly holds me and all my brother and sister Planet-Beings in our proper family relationships with one another and with Great Light. Great Light is the center for us all in our pathways. Beyond Great Light, I have heard it rumored, is a Greater Light, to which we are all bound by a tremendously powerful Still-Bigger Helper... I think sometimes I have felt..."

The quietness in Dear Earth's mind seemed to expand, expanding the boundaries of Twig's little mind as it did so. He let himself become part of that quietness, that reverence and mystery. He waited. Dear Earth waited.

Then Dear Earth seemed to return softly to her usual gentle self with a little sigh of - was it fulfillment? - and told Twig very softly, "Remember that little glimpse, dearie. It is precious and will mean much to you as you mature still more."

Twig was thinking, "*Mature*! That is what I am becoming, not a Twig any more, but a *Maturing*!" For simplicity, however, he could still just think of himself as "Twig-mind."

19. THE DOMAIN OF THE FUTURE

At times Twig still puzzled over what he was now, since he felt he was not a Twig any longer, yet certainly knew he was still himself. Dear Earth seemed to know his confusion.

"Dearie, have you considered what you would like to become in the next Domain? It is not yet firmed up, because you need to choose what Direction you want to turn your Life Forces into. The Future is being formed by your decisions and actions in the Present, you know."

"You mean I can choose what I want to be? What I'll become?"

"Yes, dearie, within your own reasonable limits. What is your dream, your desire?" Twig's mind went rushing through the parts of the universe he had thus far contacted. So many possibilities! So many choices! What out of all these did he most desire?

Then in his mind he felt Tree's presence. His own terribly hurt Tree. Without a moment's hesitation now he told Dear Earth, "To help Tree be well again."

"A good choice, dearie, a really fine decision. This means that you will become part of Big Tree-Mind, adding your own gifts about Buds and Sprouts and Leaves, to help Tree become strong and healthy again."

As she described Tree in the Future, Twig-mind saw what she described - he *saw* Tree, as he had never *seen* before, as with a new faculty that had just now erupted in him! Always before he had felt Tree, sensed Tree, known Tree's thoughts, tasted the flavors and received the rich nourishments of Tree's sap, but never until now had he *seen* like this! The picture in his mind amazed him.

"Well, dearie, this Domain is a wonderful one, isn't it, a larger one than you have known before." There was that chuckly feeling inside him, Dear Earth smiling at him tenderly again. "Just wait - there are still more Domains, each one wonderful."

Twig-mind was only half listening. He was examining the pictures in his mind, comparing the tall nice-looking Tree of the Past with the chopped-off, lop-sided Tree of the Present and the improved Tree of the Future, and eagerly plotting what Changes could be made to restore Tree as soon as possible to beauty once more. Well, maybe not really beauty, but more graceful contours, anyway.

He concentrated so one-pointedly that he was surprised when a thought

45

spoke to him. "Well, Twig! Good to have you here."

Twig-mind recognized the presence. "Branch, old Branch! Glad you found us!"

"Many of us Branches are here, getting ready to help as soon as Big Tree-Mind tells us what we are to do. What are you going to do?" asked Branch.

"I keep seeing that big wound where Biggest Branch was cut off. It is so exposed, so open to dust and all. I'd like to make sprouts all around it in a ring, to hide and protect it for Tree." In his mind he saw that circle of healthy young sprouts already growing, reaching upward with many Leaves spread out, decorating rather than hiding that huge place.

"Well, not too many of them or they will crowd each other and have to stay small," cautioned Branch.

Instantly the picture in Twig's mind eliminated half the sprouts and saw the rest growing tall, slender, strong. It amazed Twig, the way things could Change so quickly and easily!

"It's this new Domain we are in," Branch told him. "What you *think* becomes real. What you *desire* becomes real, too. You'll get used to it. We are to make Choices in this Present for Tree, so we can work with Big Tree-Mind and bring the Changes into reality in Tree's Future, *see?*"

Twig felt like nodding, though he only half understood what Branch was telling him. It did seem as if the Universe was immensely larger than he had ever conceived of - and he had felt this way over and over!

For now, however, he wanted to focus on where he would suggest new Buds to grow, in a circle around that great wound in Tree - not too many, just enough for Future beauty. He knew about Buds! He knew about Sprouts, too! His knowledge would be useful!

A new phase was beginning for him, this mind-that-used-to-be-Twig (as he thought of himself now). When Branch had teased him, asking what he called himself now that he wasn't a Twig any longer, he really didn't know what to reply. It didn't seem to matter. It wasn't important what his name was or what he called himself - maybe just "Twig-mind." The important thing was the work that needed to be done for Tree, who was still in the Time Domain and still hurting.

It was new for him to find himself in close mental communication with many other Twigs, all of them, like himself, waiting for orders from Big Tree-Mind, just as Branch and all other branches and twigs of Tree used to wait for orders from Tree-as-a-whole. There was a nice feeling of cooperation, a oneness of purpose, a sort of - well, he had heard People use the word "Brotherly" to mean a closeness of feelings. Maybe he felt that the other Twigs and Branches were his brothers. He felt that he was a group member and had become larger by that Change. He had felt it once before, when for an instant he felt himself become one part of Tree-as-a-whole. It was nice, working together with them all, for the one purpose.

Twig's mind focused steadily on that circle where he wanted new buds to grow. How was this to be done?

Branch's thought counseled him. "Just *visualize* a Bud under the bark near the sap vessels, and keep *thinking* of it and *seeing* it begin to grow," Branch advised.

"What's '*visualize*'?" asked Twig. Then he remembered, "Oh, yes, that new '*seeing*' thing that we can do now! You mean I should '*see*' the Bud there, where there isn't any Bud? That wouldn't be true. It wouldn't be real."

"Not in the Time Domain - that is, not *yet*. But the 'seeing' is like a pattern for the Future, get it? Tree can't see or feel a Bud there yet, not until you make a pattern for one with your 'visualization' and your thought, and your wish to have one grow into a nice tall Sprout. Thoughts and desires are what make things real in this Domain, remember. The patterns make an itchy place that Tree knows is a Bud wanting to form, so Tree goes ahead and sends Life Forces and makes a Bud. *Now do you get it?*"

"Hm. So my '*visualization*' and my *thought* and my wanting a Bud make a pattern that itches?"

"Oh, for twiggish sakes, Twig! Be sensible. The *pattern* doesn't itch, it makes Tree feel an itch. That attracts Tree's attention. It feels the same way a Bud does when it starts to form, so Tree starts one." He paused. "You'll get the hang of it soon. This is the way we work in this Domain. I have been Down before, a good many times, so this is old stuff for me now."

His thoughts to Twig were not cross nor critical, merely explanatory. Later Twig felt that Branch was speaking like a wise helpful older "brother" to a younger "brother." That was a rather nice feeling!

20. DOMAIN OVERLAP. TREE'S PHANTOM LIMBS

The days of the Big Cold passed one after the other. Tree had remained

47

numb for many weeks, the raw wounds dry, the sap from Root sluggish, moving only enough to continue the development of the Buds and Branches remaining.

As the Warm Time began, Root became more active, sucking more water from Dear Earth and sending it up more quickly.

Tree became responsive to the orders coming now from Big Tree-mind: "Ignore the large wounds for now except to form Buds where indicated. Focus on the Branches remaining, create new Buds and Sprouts to form large Leaves to replace the Leaf-Buds lost."

Twig concentrated on his own chosen task. Carefully he plotted where each Bud should be placed, carefully he visualized it growing, the waxy sheath being pushed open by the pressure of the swelling Bud inside, then the sprouting of the slender stem and tiny leaflets. He felt that he was pouring his own Life Forces into each Bud as it grew.

"Yes, you are, but in a different Domain, a different level of Life, dearie," came the familiar voice. "You are nurturing the Buds with your Thought-energies, your intention, your patience and perseverance, and your great steady Desire-energies for Tree to be healed. Good working, dearie."

"What is the new Domain, Dear Earth?"

"Hard to describe, dearie, except as I just did: It doesn't concern forms and bodies, as Big Tree-mind does and, of course, the entire Time Domain. It concerns feelings, intent, motivation, purpose, and such. There is a division in the Feeling Domain as in the Mental Domain - one part concerns the feelings and purposes that cause destruction and pain, deprivation, cruelty - " (Dear Earth's thoughts were sad and heavy here,) "but the other part concerns the feelings that you have been having yourself, dearie - the happiness and joy of knowing that you are helping one needing help, the knowledge that you are useful, valuable, and valued. And loved."

At this last word the warm sweet feeling inside of Twig grew so large and bright and clear that he felt he would surely burst into another creature entirely! He felt Dear Earth's kindly smile like a hug, a kiss. And he loved her, too, as much as he could possibly love...

"Yes, dearie, this Domain is full of things that make us expand and become greater, more inclusive, more understanding. We have to begin with our first little selves, just as you did as a Bud and as I did as a Nebula, and then gradually grow, develop, evolve, mature... and eventually become something else, something greater."

"One reminder, dearie," she finished, "you will need to grow Patience toward Tree and your Buds, because things in the Time Domain do *take Time to change*, remember. Part of your development now will be to grow in steadiness, firmness of intent, patience, and perseverance - all those good things that People talk about, and talk about, and keep trying to be!

"My People-children, too, are still evolving, dearie, just like you and me."

In the Time Domain everything had been slow during the Big Cold, including the adjustments that Tree was making. Root was a great consolation during this period, for Root continued his constant, deliberate activities and acted as a stabilizing factor for all of Tree, although Root himself felt the shock of that terrible Change.

"Thanks to you, Root, we'll get through all the Changes necessary," Trunk sent the message Down. "It is good that the People did not disturb you, as they did the Roots of those other Trees when they dug that ditch to lay more of their wire-things in it. They chopped many of those Roots in two, and the Trees are handicapped now and may have to let some Branches go."

Root didn't reply in so many thoughts but sent back a strong, steady sense of persistence and assurance. Translated, it would be, "Yes, I am keeping on with my job. Don't worry."

The Upward parts of Tree, however, couldn't keep from worrying. That stub of Biggest Branch, especially, still was raw. Twig began to perceive that something was different about it.

Focusing with his new talent of seeing in the Past he saw Biggest Branch there, complete, as before the day of destruction. He re-focused and still saw Biggest Branch there, but rather shadowy.

Puzzled, for his mind knew that Biggest Branch had been detached from Trunk and then sawed up and the pieces taken away, he focused on Tree in the Present. Yes, he saw the sawed-off stub and saw a shadowy Biggest Branch extending from it.

Then he focused to see into the Future Domain. This was still unfamiliar but he tried, and again he saw that complete but shadowy Biggest Branch and some others that had been cut off. This was a Question he really did have to ask. Would Air know?

No, Air ignored him.

Did Dear Earth know?

Dear Earth responded, "Dearie, Tree's *Energy-body* hasn't yet accepted

49

that Biggest Branch and the others are now detached and gone. The detached Branches are still attached to Tree through the Energy Patterns of their Life Forces. These Life Forces hold onto the Energy Pattern that is now Past. There wasn't enough time for Tree to withdraw the Life Energies from the Branches that he knew the People were going to cut off: Otherwise these ghosts wouldn't be here. I'll speak to Tree.

"Tree, dear, what does your Biggest Branch need? What does it tell you?"

"It keeps telling me it hurts. It is a big part of me, Dear Earth, and it feels uncomfortable and congested and it hurts. Some other Branches, too, keep tingling or itching and I don't know what to do about them."

"Yes, People came and detached Biggest Branch along with those others, remember? Turn your Tree-mind back, dear, and think how it was - without sadness. Be brave!"

There was a pause. Slowly Tree sent his answer back, "Then what is this great limb that is here now, where Biggest Branch always was before? And the other Branches? *I feel them.*"

"They need to have their Energy Bodies made comfortable with the Present so that they don't cause you discomfort in any way. I'll ask Big Tree-mind to have Moving massage the places where Biggest Branch and the others used to be in the Time Domain. Tree, dear, you can tell Moving where to touch and stroke the ghost-limbs. Moving should make forceful strokings at first, from their attachment to Trunk outward toward the tips of the Branches, just as if they were still there in the time Domain. Later Moving can massage more gently. You will find that this helps you to feel better. And, dear, you might think how funny it is, really, that you have *Ghost-Branches*!"

(Dear Earth was murmuring to herself, "This is more complicated than when that man-person's leg was severed by a rail-car in that tunnel the People were digging under the mountains. The man-person still felt that his limb was always very cold. When other persons dug up the man's buried limb and put it behind a warm stove the man-person no longer felt that coldness.")

"What about all these smaller Branches that still itch like crazy, Dear Earth?" came the desperate thought from Tree. "I know they were sawed off, but I still feel them!"

"Try seeing them in your mind held up high into the *cool* Air and some

50

cooling Raindrops coming Down to cool them. Also, think to yourself that you are drawing in the pure healing *coolness* of Air and sending it like sap all through your ghost-limbs and then pushing it out of the ends of your Branches along with all those uncomfortable feelings. Keep thinking that; make it real. Change the cool to *warm* if *warm* feels better. Don't spend Time in feeling sad that you are no longer complete, dear. I'll ask Air to help you."

She paused, as Tree began to follow her directions.

"Now, dear Tree, have you looked bravely at the Past? Then look now bravely at the Present, even though it is painful to you. Feel all of your Life Forces and faithful Root now working to renew your health under the wise guidance of Big Tree-mind, who has had many experiences like yours to deal with. Big Tree-mind knows what you need. Don't you sense his presence?

"And now look into the Future, dear. Much improvement has been accomplished, and your own Tree-mind has learned much in courage, adaptability, perseverance. All of these have become part of Big Tree-mind, a great and valuable addition to his total wisdom."

Tree, full of his own hurts and mutilations, had been only half aware of Dear Earth's proffered thoughts at first, then he began to listen and follow her suggestions that he focus on the Present, then on the Future, and to "be brave."

Twig-mind was aware of this Change. Tree was accepting the Present, even with its distortions and limitations, and was ready to begin, with courage, the long work of recovery, knowing he had help.

"Persevere - be patient - have courage." Tree kept the thoughts in his Tree-mind constantly, during the Dark Times as well as the Bright Times. With the assistance of Big Tree-mind he chose the spots where new Buds could produce the longest new Branches and focused his Life Energies on those places.

When the new slender Branches sprouted, Tree had already selected the sites for new Leaf-buds on each of them, and then focused his Life Energies on the Leaf-buds, too. Even on the old Branches of all sizes Tree managed to produce extra Twig-buds and Leaf-buds, and all of them were nourished by faithful Root.

Season after season Tree followed this routine, following a pattern given by Big Tree-mind, attempting to restore the shape and contours of his own kind. The original pattern could not be restored but much improvement was gradually accomplished as Dear Earth moved around Great Light time after time.

21. YEARS PASS, THEN A GREATER COMING-DOWN

Then there came a time when Tree felt a second shocking thought-blow from someone. The shock spread instantly throughout Tree-as-a-whole. This thought was that Tree was to be cut down so that the Road could be made wider, and Trunk would be sawed up for lumber.

"*Lumber*? What is that?" Tree-as-a-whole steeled himself for the terrible process of the sawing. He already knew what *sawing* was. The sawing was dreadful, and this time Root was being severed from the rest of Tree. The Up parts of Tree would be cut off from nourishment and would become "lumber," whatever that was.

Twig-mind watched from within Big Tree-mind while the People-creatures cut down Trunk, sawed off the Branches close to Trunk, and took them all away. He followed as Cars and Trucks took Trunk to a place full of Tree smells and People things, and watched while Trunk and many other Trunks from other Trees were sawed into slabs of "lumber," the slabs smoothed, placed into great piles, and left there, exposed to Air, Light, and Rain, without Bark for protection or Buds for the Future. Twig-mind couldn't help feeling a helpless, deep sadness.

"Think like the People, dearies," breathed a thought.

So Tree-mind and Twig-mind focused outside themselves into the People-minds of the People who came to see those piles of "lumber." Some of them felt eager and happy. They made Talk-noises that meant they were planning a Nest for themselves in the Future Domain, and they needed this "lumber" to make the Nest - also much other material that they made talk-noises about. They did seem eager and cheerful.

Twig-mind could see into the Future Domain more easily now. He focused on the Future of Tree - and saw dimly a neat little House with a couple of adult People and some Larvae living in it happily.

"They call it a *Home*," he felt Dear Earth tell him. She seemed to feel happy too.

These cheery emotions from the People helped Twig-mind to let go more of his sadness. He felt himself almost understanding some of those

52

LOUISE IRELAND-FREY, M.D.

strange People-creatures!

During these years the awareness-that-used-to-be-Twig became accustomed to the freedom to see, to think, to receive thoughts about his own kind of Tree and wider knowledge of other kinds of Trees. When he let himself contact Bigger Tree-mind, his awareness could reach out to Trees of all kinds in the Time Domain, from tiny seedlings and little saplings to even old blighted trees, all over Dear Earth, a wonderful yet sometimes a sad awareness. It was confusing at first to let his awareness spread throughout many different kinds of Trees. So he would simply focus his thought on one certain kind of tree, and he would be in its Big Tree-mind...

He asked many Questions and received Answers from many sources. One of his favorite sources was Bigger Tree-mind. It was with a feeling of startlement, a thrill, that he finally realized that *now he was a part of Bigger Tree-mind* - just as once, as tiny Twig, he had felt himself a part of Tree! "Littles into Bigs, and Bigs to Littles," he remembered being told. Oh, yes!

22. THE KINGDOMS, AND DEAR EARTH'S STORY

After learning much in this realm of Tree-minds, he then expanded into the still greater realm of the minds of other Plant-beings like Bushes, Grasses, one-season-Plants, and many-season-Plants. Dear Earth told him that People called this realm *Plant Kingdom.*

She sent him that smiley feeling again. "Some of my children puzzle the People. They don't know whether they are Plants or Animals. Then -" she chuckled, "then the Plant-studying People, the *Botanists*, used to study all Plants except such as these; and the Animal-Studying People, the *Zoologists*, used to study all Animals except these... so these were ignored by all those Life-Studying People, those Biologists! They are getting around to them finally."

"*Animals*? Are those the Rootless Beings?"

"Most Animals are rootless, yes. Most land-Animals have Legs and Walk or Run, but others live in water, and instead of Legs they have Fins or move through the water by other means. People call these living creatures on land or in the water *Animal Kingdom.*"

Dear Earth did not send these thoughts directly into Twig's mind but rather surrounded his Twig-mind with the cloud of this new knowledge, so

53

that he might absorb as much as he was able to, knowing that everything was here to be comprehended as he matured enough, evolved enough, to do so. And indeed his Twig-mind did keep on expanding - and still asking Questions!

"Are the People-creatures 'Animals'? They are Rootless."

Dear Earth sent a burst of laughter into his mind. "Ah, little one, you have touched a tender spot in People's *Psyche*, the People-mind. They have great arguments among themselves about that very thing. Actually, the answer is Yes and also No. Their bodies, their Time Domain forms, are Rootless Animal bodies, yes, and need the same things that other animal bodies do. They also have many of the same basic patterns of emotions and feeling-responses that other animals do.

"However, Big People-mind has developed their thinking-apparatus more than other Animals - that is, they have developed farther in the Mind Domain, beyond the Time Domain. They think into the Future and call it Planning and Foresight; and they preserve portions of the Past and call it History - things like that. So People give themselves a name for themselves alone, and call themselves *Human Kingdom*. Actually they are quite a *different* Kingdom, dividing themselves into many groups, even sometimes forgetting that they are just more of my dear Children." And Dear Earth sighed, a long, wistful sigh.

Twig-mind thought a long time about the three Kingdoms. He tried to *visualize* the Kingdoms as Circles with their edges overlapping a little. Maybe the people creatures really were partly of both Kingdoms? He tried to send his Twig-mind into each Circle, but was totally confused by the overwhelming complexity in each one. His mind withdrew to observe and just think about it. Well, he would ask Dear Earth. She wouldn't be cross about another Question.

It seemed that Dear Earth already sensed his Question, for she showed him the Circles that he had visualized, with quiet, tender amusement, "Dearie, I think your Twig-mind is in the part of the Plant-Kingdom Circle that overlaps with the Human-Kingdom Circle! You seem to like Diagrams. And so do the Human Creatures. They love Diagrams!"

Twig-mind might once have been taken aback. Now he only said, "Tell me please, Dear Earth, what do you mean? I never was a People!"

"No, dearie, you have always been a Plant-Being. Now look, I'll show you another Kingdom." She made a large circle form in Twig-mind's awareness, a

Circle that surrounded all the other three. "This is *The Mineral Kingdom*. In the Time Domain this is the first of the Kingdoms, the first one I formed after my Nebulahood was past.

"Oh, my infancy was wild and my adolescence was crazy! First surrounded by the hot gases, feeling Helper smash things onto my skin until I had grown quite a large body then cooling enough to let Water-as-vapor condense out of Air into enormously thick Clouds that absorbed all the Light from Great Light; and then eons of getting Water-as-vapor changed into Water as-liquid and having it drawn Down by Helper in torrents of Rain."

Dear Earth paused.

"Helper didn't *smash* things onto me any more than I *drew* things to me by Helper. That is the way it was. When I was a Nebula, little things swam around and if we got close to one another we just stayed close, and after a while we became a larger thing that drew other things more strongly - and that *drawing* was Helper. When I grew large Helper also had become large and drew things powerfully, so it felt to me as if they smashed onto me. Poor things, what they must have felt, grabbed and thrown hard at me!

"That was long ago... With Helper's assistance I now had an earth-body and it was made of 'minerals' - some parts solid, others liquid, others gaseous, but all called aspects of the *Mineral Kingdom*. I thought I could never like anything more than I loved Minerals."

Twig-mind was very still. He wanted Dear Earth to continue the story of her life. He was almost afraid to think this thought, lest it interrupt hers.

"Then, after eons of *revolving* around Great Light, all this while *rotating* my body on my axis as was natural to me, I began to become educated a bit at a time, and realized that a Big Helper was holding me to Great Light and that was why I was moving around him. I could feel his centripetal pull, steady, powerful, irresistible - and somehow, as an adolescent, I resented it and wanted to get away! I laugh, now! But my desire made me focus my mind on getting away from Great Light, and I began to understand that my very desire was a Force, a Centrifugal force. Great Light understood perfectly and counteracted exactly, so that he drew me in a circle, letting me have a certain freedom while still holding me in his Family.

"It was after I had settled down somewhat from all the Changes of my early eons that I realized how huge I had become and also what enormous responsibilities had become mine. By then my Earth-mind had grown, too. I decided to divide my Earth-mind into parts and assign each part a problem to focus on, or a Plan for a Future to develop."

Dear Earth paused.

"That was when I really began to mature, dearie. First I focused on Minerals, of course, and assigned one part of my mind to considering and evolving fire-related rocks, now called *igneous* ones. Other parts of my mind I assigned to other types, such as *crystalline* types. That was such a pleasure! It was a delight to see what Crystal-mind would come up with! Crystal-mind, of course, felt at first that she was just herself, and only later came to understand that she was an integral part of me - just as you are doing, dearie.

"Eons later it occurred to me that there might be other ways to express the great Forces, so I began assigning mind-parts to create patterns for water-dwelling bodies that could sustain Life, Plants of that early Time, and then simple land-dwelling Animal bodies... Those were exciting eons in the Time Domain!

"And all this is still here, dearie, in my Beyond-Time Memory. I showed you a glimpse once. It is still here.

"Now look, see what your Diagram needs, to show the Mind/Feeling Domain."

Twig-mind watched as his Circles reappeared, then saw that each was actually a sort of sphere rounding up into a new dimension. Each sphere was like a bumpy irregular bubble, the Thought or Mind-part.

"In the Future the 'bubbles' will become perfect spheres, interlacing delicately as you see the Circles overlapping a bit in the center now, but in this Present they look as you see them here with irregularities and imperfections. Feelings and emotions are closely linked with mind-thoughts and color them, as you see. Some are beautiful, some are not. Not for quite a long Time yet."

Washes of color swam over and through the spheres, streams of color, many dark streams and splotches but also many streams of bright colors and sparkles of light. "These are 'diagrams,' we might say, of the Thoughts and Feelings of all my children at Present."

Although Twig-mind was fascinated by all this new knowledge, a more personal Question insisted on being asked: "If as you say I am partly in Human Kingdom, will I ever become a People?" he asked

"No, dearie, I was teasing you. You belong in Plant Kingdom, as do all other Beings in your Plant Life-Wave. Only when this entire Cycle is ended

Will your *Life-Wave* move on into a 'higher' Life Wave and you become members of a new Animal Kingdom, so I am told. The Beings in Animal Kingdom of this Present will be in Human Kingdom then, and the present People will be in a higher one yet, the Spiritual Kingdom. This applies to the Mind-Souls, not the bodies. The bodies in the Time Domain will have various forms."

"Even now, I perceive, some of the People-minds are struggling out of the Human into the Spiritual Kingdom. Their bodies still look like Human bodies, their Minds still have mostly Human thoughts and feeling; but their Higher Minds are expanding, stretching, evolving - just as you in a smaller way have been expanding, dearie. It is the natural way for all the Life Waves. We all continue to grow. Isn't it a wonderful Pattern?"

The next Question almost burst out. "Is there a *Biggest* Mind that makes the Pattern? Such a BIG pattern!"

Dear Earth became very quiet, reverent as she had once when Twig had asked about a Biggest Helper.

"Dear, I believe there is. At times I have felt sure of it. I *am* sure of it."

23. LIGHT, AND GREAT LIGHT'S STORY

"Is Light an Allness?" Twig-mind asked one day, feeling the warmth of the light from Great Light and sensing the delight and joy with which the Plants of the Plant Kingdom basked in it. Yet there were also drifts of other feeling; like a gasping for breath or a shriveling from too much heat, like memories from the Past, or like wafts of feelings from Distance.

"Well - Yes, and then in certain ways No," answered Dear Earth. "Why don't you ask your Question of Light itself?"

Instantly Twig-mind found that he was streaking along a Light-ray toward Great Light, which was growing larger and more dazzling every nanosecond.

"Wait, wait, wait! Stop, stop! I can't - I just can't - - " he managed to send out. Instantly everything slowed.

"A Question came from the Earth direction. I was taking it to Great Light to be answered," explained Light. "I am only a Ray, and Rays are like an Allness. Light itself is..." The answer trailed off. "Ask Great Light."

"How do I reach Great Light?"

A sense of being surrounded in an enormous "Granule" of energies engulfed Twig-mind.

"Ah, a little Earth-soul. We heard your Question. Yes, Light-rays are indeed like an Allness. I send out my energies, and they streak out in all directions as Light and other things in different frequencies. These keep on shooting out through the Time-Distances of the Time Domain until they reach something - something like an Earth, or maybe a Twig."

"Even things so - so - so little?" stammered Twig-mind.

"That is why Light is an Allness. It shines on everything, touches and warms everything, but may also damage things if it shines too long or heats something too much. It is not a <u>who</u>, it is an <u>it</u>, not trying to help anything but not intending to hurt, either. It is an Allness, and can be a friend and assistant if the laws it follows are obeyed."

"Oh, yes, that is what we learned about Helper, too," Twig-mind replied, remembering what Helper had done to the little Crow nestling who had fallen from her nest.

"But you, Great Light, are a Being. How can you make an Allness that isn't you?"

Almost Twig-mind felt as he did when Dear Earth was amused at him. This Granule of Great Light was smiling at him, just as she did - and with that same gentleness, that tender teasing, now magnified into the mega-dimension. It wasn't frightening but it was - well, overwhelming.

"Yes, my daughter Earth told me about your Questions, little Earth-soul. She is probably correct, that your soul is in that part of your Animal Kingdom diagram that overlaps with the Human Kingdom Circle. Human creatures do ask lots of Questions. Oh, yes, oh, yes!"

This time the amusement extended to include the entire Kingdom of People, a huge solar plexus laughter. "We let them learn a good many things. They are very inventive, very probing, very inquisitive. Sometimes too much so for their own good or for my daughter Earth.

"She can take care of herself but it is hard for her, and of course hard on her children of all Kingdoms. She took on a tremendous responsibility when she volunteered to give shelter to the souls that needed a place in which to grow and mature. Many of them are young souls that haven't evolved beyond the 'me-first' and 'my rights-my wrongs' stage in the Mind Domain."

Twig-mind felt in Great Light the same resignation and patience that he had felt in Dear Earth. Then he remembered how he himself had been, a little Twig aware only of himself, Branch, and his Buds, except that in his case there were also his Questions reaching out.

Great Light knew his thoughts, of course. "It is a natural stage, but often difficult." (Twig recalled Dear Earth's saying, "My adolescence was crazy.")

Great Light continued, "I, too, was once a Nebula, but my development was not like the early eons of my children, the Planets. I am held by a Greater Helper, a powerful Centripetal Force, while my own equal Centrifugal Force enables me to continue to move around - to revolve so - around a Greater Light, along with my Family. I take them all with me. We are called a Solar System - and I am the Sol." There was that mighty amusement.

"You have a *Bigger* Helper? Holding you to revolve around a *Bigger Light*?"

"Does that amaze you, Earth-soul? *Littles to Bigs, Bigs to Littles.* Ever heard that?"

"But you are so huge, so great! How could there be anything more powerful than you?"

"I understand why my Daughter enjoys your company, little one. Already you have become part of a large Plant-soul, so you understand how a small soul can expand, little by little, step by step, even through death of the Time-domain body; and beyond into the Mind-Feeling Domain, and now beginning to grow into the Soul Domain."

He paused.

"I might... you won't understand yet... but you will wonder about another Question... so I might as well give you a glimpse now..."

He softened his Light and gently decreased his heat to Twig-mind.

"How big am I, Earth-soul? Very big indeed, you may say? What if I tell you that I am just one member of a *Big Family*, called a *Galaxy*? There are many Families like mine in the Big Family, many, many! Some have more members than others. We all revolve around a *Greater Light*, held by the *Greater Helper*. We are an Extended Family, a unit, the *Galaxy*.

"Now think of our Galaxy as one among others, making a *Bigger Family*, a whole Family of Galaxies. Got it, Earth-soul? These revolve around a Center - not a Light nor a Being. It is where the Great Helpers of each of the Galaxies meet in a Center which, like a huge Greater Helper, holds all the Galaxies of this Bigger Family together. Somebody - who? - called us '*Local Group*.' Oh, yes, it may have been some of those Earth-creatures. They love names and numbers."

Twig-mind couldn't keep up with all this no matter how he tried, and he did try hard.

"Don't strain the mind, Earth-soul. Just relax the mind, stop trying, and permit the ideas to be wafted into your thoughts. That's all. No need to try to understand yet. It's okay. You are maturing. There is much Time and also Beyond-Time, you know."

Twig-mind suddenly felt like laughing, to hear Great Light send the 'okay' thought. That was what the Larvae of People say! Of course Great Light knew that - his Light Rays bathed the Larvae every time they ran into his sunlight.

He must know about things, about his other Children, too, the other Planets. Great Light knew whatever his Rays *reached*, whatever they were *reflected to*, and *whatever* they *penetrated* and were *transmitted through*. What a BIG MIND!

24. IS THERE A GREATEST LIGHT? A GREATEST HELPER?

"Well, that is a couple of things for you to ponder on, Earth-soul. The Universe goes on and on, and we '*Stars*' can communicate across Time-Space by our Rays, which criss-cross each other in Space like a fabric. If an Earth-creature can see a Star, the Star of course is seeing the Earth creature. So it is with us Stars. Our Light in the Time Domain does take Time even as swiftly as it shoots forth, so we consider this Web more like a four-dimensional blanket or Matrix. We really communicate through the Mind Domain, where thoughts fly instantaneously - no more problem with that limiting Speed-of-Light thing."

"You mean like the way Dear Earth communicates with me and her other children? She said People do something like that and call it *Telepathy*."

"Mmm, yes, but even better than that. More like the way you felt when you became part of Big Tree-mind and then part of Plant-mind. Remember that? As if you were part of an All-Awareness."

"Then, Great Light, you mean you can know-into and feel-into the knowledge and wisdom of all the other Stars that you can see? Doesn't your own Light blind you to theirs? Theirs is so tiny!"

"You have hit on another Big Question there, Earth-soul. What we Stars seem to find is that each fragment in the Universe is important in some way, either Past or Present or Future, and either for improvement or for the reverse. Size may not be important. Neither may energy be a main factor. All these are of the Time Domain. Big bright Stars live splendidly for a 'short' time in the Time Domain and then Change, whereas small, dim, or low-energy Stars tend to exist for a much longer time, have a much longer life before they Change.

"I hear your Question about a Greatest Light, little Earth-soul. I can see the rays of many, many other Stars and many other Galaxies. I have heard of other tremendously powerful Greater Helpers, and there may be a *Greatest Light* toward which perhaps we are drawn by a *Greatest Helper*, a *Great Attractor*... and yet there may be more beyond... The Universe is vast, stupendous, mysterious...

"And *all this is in the Time-Domain*. In higher Realms the Minds and Souls keep on evolving. Greatest Light is also evolving, for His Mind-Soul is expanding from the expansions of all His Children. And in the Domain of Spirit - We are all Spirit-sparks in the *Greatest Spirit*, little one."

Great Light held this thought in an immense Silence, an awe-filled Stillness. "All of us together in a Big Holy."

After a long moment he resumed, "Earth-soul, remind my little Daughter Earth that I am aware of her pains and illnesses, and of her efforts to equalize the strains and recover from the sicknesses. I sense them all, the great problems she is having to deal with. She is a courageous Being but her strength does have limits. I feel her stress. Sometimes my own stresses erupt out of my patience, too, and I understand - even though she and the other three little Planets are so *different* from the rest of us - except for the little fellow that the Big Brothers' Helper snagged and pulled in. I adopted him and his pet what-d'you-call-it."

All this was outside of Twig-mind's knowledge. He listened, just to have the thoughts inside where he could later call them back and think about them. So many Questions!

Before he could choose which Question to ask, however, Great Light's own thoughts began to mutter and churn, not to Twig-mind but to himself, or maybe to Dear Earth.

"Poor little Daughter. I felt it was all right for those People of hers, those *Astronomers* and *Mathematicians* and *Physicists*, to discover how I Shine. In fact, I felt rather proud of them, of their People-minds. I neglected to look into the Domain of the Future to see how their discovery could be so

61

horribly misused by other People-minds, how their abuse of it would hurt you, little Daughter, and destroy so much and so many in the Time-Domain when it was distorted in the Mind-Domain to unworthy uses.

"Now you are suffering severe burns from the explosions under your skin, feeling the pains and despair of the Plant and Animal Beings that have been scorched by the explosions over your skin, in *addition* to having various Earth-sicknesses that make you tremble with chills in one place, burn with fever in others, cry floods of tears in some place, while gasping with dryness in others. Many of your Children, the Plants and Animals, are suffering. I see them. Many are hurting or dying from your own efforts, as well. That is inevitable, I know. It is a Time of your Changing.

"Dear little Daughter, I feel your weariness. You are doing the best you can. Just keep on."

The thoughts ceased as specific thoughts. There was a tremendous, boiling, sad/strong firmness in his Feeling/Mind, but his Light was steady as he sent it radiating out in all directions.

Twig-mind remained very still, engulfed in what Great Light was feeling. He had not realized that Dear Earth, always so cheery and gentle, could be feeling pain. Itches, yes, but not deep pain and sickness.

And Great Light - even he could feel strains, his own and those of his Family.

Twig-mind became aware that Great Light had turned his attention Outward toward another member of his Family. Twig-mind quietly withdrew his own attention and turned it toward Dear Earth, and, desiring to be there, found himself again in her familiar aura.

Dear Earth! She was his Home, this was where he truly belonged, not anywhere else at all. Here was his Life-Energy, and here was his work. He had helped Tree. He had helped many other Beings in Plant Kingdom. Now could he help Dear Earth? He didn't know how. And he was so small, even as part of plant Kingdom.

25. THE DIFFICULT TIMES OF CHANGING

"Dear Earth, I have another Question, an old one, really,"

"Well, dearie. I am getting pretty good at answering your Questions after all this experience."

Twig-mind smiled at the little joke but beneath Dear Earth's humor he felt an undercurrent. Was she covering up her tiredness, her sadness?

"Dear Earth, do you know *why* Storm sometimes gets so wild and terrible that he hurts Beings like Crows and Branches? *Why?* And *why* does Fire go so wild and kill so many Plant Beings and Animal Beings sometimes? And *why* do People - - "

Dear Earth mused a while. This was not like her. Usually she answered at once.

"Dearie, I am not sure there is an easy answer, certainly not a clear, direct one easy to understand. I feel that there is a Great Plan, and these events sometimes just happen to be parts of it. Part of the Plan includes my Life-processes that have to do with Air and Water, and Warmth and Currents. Great Light has his own cycles, and they affect me, too.

"When the Changes hinder or injure my children of the three Kingdoms, I am deeply sorry. In coping with these hindrances and pains or even in letting their bodies die and go Down, they do learn much and their Soul-minds grow stronger, but I am sad for their suffering. Great Light understands. He knows that Changes cause pain and these *are* Times of Changing.

"At other times it seems that People-plans conflict with other People-thoughts and erupt into Storms in the Mind/Feeling realm with Feelings of hate, anger, jealousy - all those of the lower Division of the realm. Then People rage at one another other and cause more pain, fear, and hate - the Lower Level feelings. When a cycle like this gets started it is so hard to slow it down, and it influences the Mind Realm and even the Soul Realm.

"In the Three Kingdoms, also in Human Kingdom, some of the causes of great problems are due to the overweening attitude of one type of Being over the others, a belief that it is better and more deserving than the others. The little Aphid Beings, for instance, delicate little creatures, may begin to feel that a Tree is their own possession, and may over-multiply and eventually suck the very Life-energies out of the Tree."

Twig-mind felt himself shrivel at the very thought of such greed, such cruelty.

"Or a certain Beetle may over-multiply and begin to feast on Spruce-trees, or a different Beetle may over-multiply and begin to invade a different kind such as Pinion, and the Trees may not be able to keep their Life Energies as the Beetles eat and eat under their Bark."

Twig-mind could hardly bear to hear these things. He had seen the thousands of tired, dying Trees and had felt their illness and hopelessness. He had urged them to let their Life Forces gently withdraw and let their bodies go Down.

"*Why*, Dear Earth? Is this part of that Plan you spoke about?"

"Dearie, the Aphids and the Beetles are my children, too, remember. So are the tiny Beings that People fear, called 'germs,' 'viruses,' things like that. They are all my children. They all need to be in harmony with one another, in balance, none overpowering the others, none trying to prevent the others from a Life here on my skin. They are still immature in the Feeling-Realm if they believe and act as if they are better than others and try to take more than an appropriate share of the gifts I offer. Or the gifts that others of my children can freely give them."

Twig-mind felt her sadness and frustration. The problems were so BIG!

"To be honest, dearie, I don't know all the causes of these troubles nor do I know what the solutions of them are. We all just go ahead the best we can, dearie."

26. BACK TO BRANCH AND THE LARVAE THAT ITCH.

"Dear Earth, you have helped me so much and taught me so much, now it is time for me to help you."

"And *teach* me?" She could still prod him with a thought! Twig chuckled.

"Well, I'll ask you to answer more Questions. I guess that *teaches* you patience. Will that help?" He felt rather proud of his witticism. He was learning how to tease, and she was teaching him.

"No, dearie, you still have a great deal to learn yet, and then you can help me. Now you need to practice your *feeling-into* the other Beings in Plant Kingdom. You have been granted glimpses of the Kingdoms, and Great Light gave you a Mind-Domain glimpse of the Time Domain universe. Then you chose to come back here to me.

"This is your Home, as you felt, dearie. And you are right; this is where your responsibilities and your joy are. You are maturing well, now feeling responsibility and a desire to fulfill it, no longer focused on your own adventures and your Questions. Am I close, dearie?"

Twig-mind accepted her evaluation with a seriousness that surprised him. Maybe he really was "maturing!"

"What is my next lesson, Dear Earth?' he asked. "That isn't a real Question," he added.

"To begin the practice of *feeling-into* other Beings, I suggest that you feel-into one of the Trees that is being overwhelmed by Aphids."

"No." The refusal popped out of Twig-mind with astonishing force.

"Or feel-into your own Tree, be in Branch and feel as he felt when the Larvae - - "

"NO!" Twig-mind himself was amazed at the intensity of his rejection.

Dear Earth did not seem to be surprised. Quietly she soothed his disturbance. "I understand perhaps better than you know, dearie. It is the old fear and hostility that you felt from Branch long ago when you were a little impressionable Bud and then a little ignorant Twig. Impressions received when one is very young go deep into the Mind/Feeling part of your Being, often with overlaid additional Feelings. The way to neutralize these and to comfort and heal the Mind/Feeling part is to revisit the bad events, see them with your mature vision, and let Time and new knowledge swiftly erase their power. Then your Mind/Feelings will be freed, and your Soul part will be stronger. Come now, you want to help me?"

"Yes, but - but - not like this... I mean, I do, but isn't there something else I can do for you?"

"Nothing that would help me more, dearie. I know it takes courage. I am with you, you know."

Twig-mind hesitated, thought, seized the fear in his Mind part, grasped the courage in his Feeling part, and made the two face each other in his Soul part... and then he felt once more his great Desire to help Dear Earth. That strong Desire, full of gratitude to her, was the deciding factor.

"Yes, Dear Earth. I - I will. When do I start?"

There was a tenderness in Dear Earth's answer. "You already have, dearie. Feel it?"

For a moment there was nothing - nothing but a familiar, cozy feeling of being a Twig, sending Questions and receiving Answers from a Branch. This time Branch was sending thoughts of things called Larvae that were underneath Branch's bark and were making itchy feelings there. Branch sent the thought that they were babies of Beetle-beings, and they were eating away at Branch's tissues and making the places itch and feel bad.

Twig-mind felt the thoughts from Branch as he had back then in the Time Domain, but now he felt them as Branch had felt them. He was feeling-into Branch's feelings... then into Tree's feelings... and he learned that Tree had a number of other Branches that were made itchy by the Larvae.

"They have no right!" Twig-mind's angry thought crashed against the Larvae. "They are hurting Tree, they are weakening Tree! They should not be here at all!"

Then Dear Earth's calm thought entered and swept away his anger.

"Now send your mind into the Larvae, dearie."

"No! I mean - No, I really don't want to get near them, they are hurting Tree!"

"You need to have courage, dear, as I told you. Do you have courage, do you have enough?"

Poor Twig-mind felt that he was being torn away from his maturing mind and reduced to a little Time-Domain Twig once more. But now he was full of strong bad feelings that Twig never knew.

"I'll try, Dear Earth. I'll try. But don't leave me - stay with me, please. I'm scared. I'm afraid..."

"I am with you, dear. Remember, like the Aphids, the Beetles are my children, too."

There was an instant of neutrality, then a strange awareness of a pleasant damp darkness. Twig-mind cautiously probed into the darkness and smelled a delicious smell, a flavor that made him eager to taste it. Without thinking he began to eat - and eat - and eat! It was wonderful!

Only then did he realize: his Mind was *feeling-into* the Mind/Feelings of a Beetle Larva. For a while longer he simply ate and ate, but all this while his Twig-mind, still in him, was thinking. "Why, this is just a baby. A baby Beetle? Okay, but still just a baby, and she is hungry. So she wants to eat. And here is all this good food around her - she can eat in any direction at all and get what she needs. She just wants to eat and grow!... and she doesn't know much else at all.

"She has no idea of Tree or Branch. She has no idea that she is making Branch feel itchy and bad. She doesn't know she is destroying some of his tissues. She is just ignorant, poor little thing. Not dumb, *just ignorant, not knowing.*"

Twig-mind rejoined his *Twig*-mind and saw with wider understanding that the Larva would soon be ready to Change into her next stage. This

Change was natural for all Larvae of her kind, so she was not afraid nor concerned about it, either now or for the future. She just did what was right for her, what Big Beetle-mind told all the Larvae to do. There was no hostility or malice or selfishness or cruelty - none of those Lower Feeling-Domain emotions and attitudes that Branch thought there were.

Twig-mind felt he ought to apologize to the Larva, yet he still felt sympathy for dear Branch. As for his own Twig-feelings about bad itchy things and their possible causes - well, the intensity seemed to be gone from them. He did feel freer, as Dear Earth had promised. This method did help.

If it helped him, then perhaps in a tiny way it helped Dear Earth, too.

Then a scary idea struck his mind: Would it help her if he used this way to overcome other Low division Feelings in himself? He really didn't want to propose it - in fact, he truly hoped Dear Earth hadn't heard his thought.

"Not yet, not yet!" he hurriedly added. "Wait, Dear Earth! Wait just a bit longer!"

Her answer rose warmly in him. "Now, dearie, you have Free Will, a great gift, a grave responsibility. Already you have begun to practice with it. You are doing very well dearie."

"I've already begun?"

"Yes, when you considered all the possible Choices about what you wanted to do, and you chose to help Tree, remember?"

"Oh, Dear Earth, that wasn't really a Choice! I mean, that was just what I wanted to do most."

"Yes, and that Choice was 'from the heart,' dearie - a fine choice. Some Choices may be 'from the Mind,' and some of those may seem harder - some may even seem to be what you don't really want. So it is wise to think carefully before you make a Choice and consider also the results of it."

Twig-mind couldn't help thinking to himself (and trying not to let Dear Earth hear what he was thinking) that she seemed to be getting a little bit preachy. He caught his thought and covered it up.

"Dearie, thoughts do have a way of getting out loose, don't they!" chuckled Dear Earth.

27. EXPANDING INTO PLANT KINGDOM

The next lesson that Dear Earth suggested to Twig-mind was to focus on

Plant Kingdom as a whole and describe what he saw. He saw his big Circle full of Plants of all sorts, a large portion of the Circle covered with Trees, all kinds of Trees. He looked at them fondly.

"Quite well done, dear, but this is how it really is," and he saw the Circle change into a hodgepodge of different Plants all scrambled together. Frankly, he was horrified. What a mess!

"But if we simplify by making each *Family* of Plants show like a single spot in the Circle, the size of each spot representing how many *genera* of that *Family* there are, this is how it looks." And the Circle was suddenly filled with definite small areas. "Here is the spot for Trees."

Dear Earth indicated a small area - *So small*! Twig-mind was amazed, appalled, hurt, angry - all those Lower-Division Feelings!

Dear Earth undoubtedly knew his feelings but she ignored them and continued, "Now see what the area of the Grasses shows," and she indicated a very large area that grew still larger as he watched. "The Grasses, dear, have been some of the most successful of Plant-Mind's experiments. Plant-Mind started them long before he began to experiment on Tree-forms.

"Don't be upset, dearie. I know you feel closer to Trees, because you yourself were once a Twig and part of a Tree. Naturally you feel an affinity for Trees more than for other Plant-forms. Part of your Change now, however, is for you to become more understanding of other Plant-forms. Do you see?" Her smile poked him, "*Get it, Twig*?"

Twig-mind had to smile in spite of himself. She was such a "dearie," herself.

Pensively he looked again at the Diagram. There were areas for Bushes, for Flowering Plants, for Ferns, for Algae. None of them drew his interest especially - or rather, all them did, equally. All but that area for Trees.

"Are you ready to feel-into a Tree that is feeding too many other Beings, called Parasites?"

"N--not yet," faltered Twig-mind. Then humbly he added, "I guess I'm not brave enough. Yet."

"Well, dearie, you know that being a Tree is not all sunshine and raindrops. Was it so bad when you felt-into the Beetle baby?"

"I guess maybe I could feel-into a - a - an Aphid baby?" Twig-mind firmly held his courage.

"Good compromise, dear. All right here you go."

In an instant he was one among a multitude of Beings like himself, leg-to-leg with them, body-to-body, all of them quiet, contented, feeding on nice juice. The juice tasted so good! Even though he wasn't really hungry, he wanted to go on forever just sucking up that juice, like all the others around him. Occasionally one or another of them would pull his beak up from the ground they sat on, move a little distance away, then put his beak down into the ground again. That good juice was everywhere under the thin bark they sat on. It was an underground feast just waiting to be tapped. What a sweet way to live! Later, when he had Wings, he would fly away to find Adventure and another Tree to rest on - -

Another Tree! Twig-mind clicked back into himself with a mental crash. At the same moment he felt Dear Earth's soft inquiry, "Dearie, don't you care to *feel-into* that weak little Tree? At least comfort her with your understanding?"

Without a moment's hesitation Twig-mind moved into the scrawny little Tree, felt her tiredness her weakness, the unpleasant smarting sensation on the delicate bark of her slender Trunk and Branches where the hosts of Aphids were attached by their mouth-tubes, all of them sucking up her Life Forces. She could do nothing about the situation, nothing at all. Patiently resigned, she was just waiting for Whatever, whenever it might come, some Change. It could hardly be a Change for the worse.

Twig-mind felt all this and had trouble controlling the Lower Level Feelings that almost overwhelmed him: sorrow, frustration, helpless anger toward the Aphids. No, they truly didn't have any thought of hurting her. They were like babies, even the older ones among them, the ones with Wings. They really were not malicious, not even selfishly greedy, just hungry, wanting to grow by sucking up that nourishing sap. They didn't realize that it was the Life Energy of a Tree. In fact, to them a Tree was nothing but a big storehouse of sweet juice for food.

Twig-mind turned his thoughts back to the little Tree, drooping and sick. "What can I do for her?" he asked the Question, sent it out urgently.

"Such work is part of the tasks of Great Plant-Mind and Great Animal-Mind, dearie. They have to coordinate their efforts while still fitting them in with my own large Earth plans and Earth Changes. It is not a matter of one little Tree or one horde of Aphids, though perhaps I can impress a People to notice the needs of little Tree here and do something to help her.

"It would be a Choice between cutting down the little Tree, as your Tree was cut down, or else of destroying the bodies of the thousands of Aphids attached to her so that she could rebuild her Life Energies once more, with the help of Big Tree-mind - including your help, dear. Which would you choose?"

Poor Twig-mind! Dear Earth felt his distress, as of course she also felt the Tree's feelings.

"Life Energies come into bodies in the Time Domain sometimes with a heavy price, dearie. This situation is part of the task that I delegated to Plant-Mind and Animal-Mind.

"Great Animal-mind needs to be reminded now that Aphid-mind has over-multiplied his bodies here, and allow balance to be restored again. If any Plant or Animal over-multiplies, balance is lost, harmony is lost. There are problems that must be faced and solved before things can be restored, and the restoration may be harsh at times. As I said before, dearie, Life in the Time Domain isn't all sunshine and raindrops."

She added, "Plant-mind has also experimented with letting some Plants parasitize others."

Twig-mind could hardly believe this! One Plant weaken another by draining its Life-energy?!

"Yes; some of these, growing on the Branches of Trees, send tendrils through the Bark and into the veins, sucking up the good sap of the Tree, and from it derive their own Life and make beautiful blossoms - flowers that are admired and sought by the Bees as well as by many People."

How could Dear Earth talk like that about *Trees*! She seemed so heartless about Trees!

"Others, also growing on the limbs of Trees, form little nest-like bunches of greenery that produce berries. Still others choose not Trees but other Plants to parasitize, growing long, leafless, bright-orange, threads from their attachments to living weeds. People-Larvae call the tangles 'Angel Hair.'"

"But, Dear Earth, it doesn't seem fair that a Tree or a Plant works to get its own Life Forces from its Root and then have its Forces sucked away by some other Plant! That's just not fair!"

"Animal-Mind has also made such experiments. A Wasp-mother, after digging a safe hole for her eggs may then sting and paralyze a Larva-caterpillar of some other insect, fly with it or drag it to that hole, and lay her eggs on it, so that her own tiny grub-larvae can eat it after they hatch. Animal-Mind and Plant-Mind have made many different experiments during all the eons

LOUISE IRELAND-FREY, M.D.

since I turned over those parts of my Earth-Mind to them and delegated the work to each of them. Many of their experiments have tuned out amazingly well. But sometimes they have created creatures that were - well - - " She paused. This sadness was an almost constant undercurrent now. She felt the stresses of her children.

She *cared* so deeply about all her children. The struggles and conflicts between them, their rivalries and competition she accepted as natural aspects of their growth, but she wished that the aspects of the Lower Feeling Domain were less prominent, less hurtful.

At the same time she knew that her own necessary Changes often injured or destroyed the bodies of many of her children. In the Time Domain, Life really isn't "all sunshine and raindrops." Sometimes Nature, as an Allness, caused fierce Heat, Or raging Floods, Wild-fires, Earthquakes, terrific Storms. These all affected her children. Sometimes, too, they affected People so much that the People's Minds and Feelings seemed to take on those same characteristics of fierce Heat, raging Hate, Cruelties, or terrible Depression and Despair - -

Rays from Great Light came and gently spread warmth over a wide area of her body. Great Light knew of her distress in the midst of his own enormous problems. With renewed courage Dear Earth turned to dealing with hers.

28. MINERAL KINGDOM AND DEAR EARTH'S HISTORY

Twig-mind had more Questions, but he made himself wait until Dear Earth had gradually become less sad. Then he asked softly, "Dear Earth, do you think that it was easier back when you were in your Bud - I mean your Nebulahood? Before you had Plant-Mind and Animal-Mind?"

"Oh, each stage has its own beauties and its own problems, dearie. Back before Plant-Mind and Animal-Mind, when I was still growing and still had a softish body, my Helper was also growing and becoming very strong. When Helper felt tiny things far away from us, he invited them to come closer. Most of them came willingly until they entered Air, which resisted their coming with Friction and Heat. The little ones burned up."

"You mean they gave up their Life Energies?"

"They didn't have Life as you think of it, dearie, they were Mineral

71

Objects that had been wandering around in Space, far beyond Air and Helper, until Helper coaxed them to come closer. It was when a few large ones came close and Helper pulled them toward me faster and faster - those were the ones that I remember vividly. Helper was clear out of his mind, except that he doesn't have a Mind! I knew that, but it was frightening to know that a big Thing was being pulled toward me so hard and so swiftly - and I could do nothing to avoid it. Helper pulled that Thing into me so hard that it went deep into my body. My skin melted, the rocks around that place were burning, they shot up into Air, and Air itself seemed to be on fire. Terrible Movings rushed here and there. Air and Water were in turmoil. Heat seared everything, everything was burning. Air was filled with smoke, soot, ash - befouled so much that Rays from Great Light could not get through to me at all for - oh, several times I went clear around Great Light.

"It got *so cold* under those black clouds of smoke and trash and soot! I shivered and froze, and so did my remaining children with me. Many of them had lost their bodies in that first dreadful Fire-time. Now many more gave up their Life Energies during the black Cold-time. When Helper at last got much of the debris in Air settled Down, and Air allowed Light to reach me again, I had to take time to see what Changes had occurred and what we might do to repair things.

"That was when Animal-Mind and Plant-Mind discovered how many of their Creatures had been destroyed. I told them to start inventing new Creature-forms, and to protect and nurture the old Forms that had survived and help them to evolve into new strong Forms.

"At first they were disconsolate, mourning the loss of their favorite Creatures. But actually I was rather relieved that some of those Creatures were gone. Some of the Plants had grown so dense that they had overgrown many smaller ones; and some of the Animals had become so gigantic and eternally hungry that they had evolved great claws and teeth to rip apart other Animals, and they spent much of their lives doing just that.

"It was the beginning of a new time, so I advised Plant-Mind and Animal-Mind to focus on bringing forth new Forms better fitted to a new, widely varied Age. It was the cataclysm of that large Object that Helper pulled into me so violently that started this Change.

"There were a few other events rather like this, and a few that were slower, more gradual, due to some of my own physiologic Changes in Air currents, Water currents, Climate Changes, and such. And then there was that terrible Change long, long before... I don't like to think back to it, dearie. That is why I understood when you didn't want to think back to the time when Branch was telling you of Beetle larvae."

She continued slowly, "So I just call that time by a name I made up: I just call it my *Discontinuity*, when practically all the Creatures of Plant-Mind and Animal-Mind, primitive as they were back then, were destroyed. We started all over. I had Mineral-Mind working to get Air and Clouds and Rain to help restore things as much as possible, so that Plants and Animals could live again. As soon as the climate on my skin was settled enough, Plant-Mind and Animal-Mind really got busy. Each of them divided itself into parts, each part to specialize on evolving a series of new Creatures, such as Plants that gradually learned to produce flowers, or little animal forms that were given a stiff cord in the back that was eventually evolved into a backbone and started a whole new complex series of Animal-forms."

Twig-mind had listened with concentration but could barely half understand all this. Now he knew why it was that Dear Earth had understood his own reluctance to go back into the Past and relive the events, or to feel-into other Creatures and sense their feelings of pain and helplessness.

Softly he asked, "Is that the hardest time you ever had, Dear Earth?" As soon as the thought was out of his mind he wished he could call it back! Why had he asked that? Such a Question would only make Dear Earth focus more intensely on this or another difficult event in her life!

"Well, dear, I'd say so, except for the time long, long before when I was still soft-bodied, not long after ceasing to be Nebulous, when my Helper, already very strong, persuaded a large passing Body to curve toward me. Helper, being an Allness, couldn't perceive that he and the Helper of the other Body would draw us together so powerfully. We side-swiped each other! A great portion of me was knocked off as we collided, but the other Body kept on, shooting off on a slightly different pathway. The part of me that had been knocked off went at an angle through Air and on into Space, and gradually became rounded to a sphere. It is still there, dearie - the Lesser Light, that we call Moon."

"Moon is the 'Lesser Light?' You haven't talked much about Lesser Light."

"Well, that is because Moon doesn't really give Light, dear. Moon receives Light from Great Light it then reflects part of it on to me - and of

73

course out in all other directions as well. Moon looks to us a Lesser Light but has no Shining of her own. Moon is lovely, though, isn't she? She's my Daughter.

"Hm. Here I have gone on and on about my own personal history. You really have no need of all this information, dearie, but if it is interesting to you or answers some of your Questions, it is all right. Now how about getting back to your rightful work in your rightful place in Big Plant-Mind?"

She actually seemed a bit embarrassed to have talked so long about her history. Twig-mind hurried to reassure her, "Oh, Dear Earth, thank you for telling me all this! I am so glad to know!"

She responded playfully, "Now get along with you, dearie. How about asking Big Plant-Mind your questions from now on? There is plenty for you to learn from him."

"All right, I will, but will you tell me first some more about People Kingdom? Everyone says that they are so complicated. Even Great Light said that."

"Can't get away from your Questions, can I, dearie? Well, yes, the Human Kingdom..."

29. HUMAN KINGDOM - AND PEOPLE

Dear Earth shivered ever so slightly. Twig-mind wondered whether she felt chilly at the very thought of the People Kingdom, or what.

"Well, if we were to show Human Kingdom on your Circle Diagram, dear, it would be a tiny circle up here inside the big Circle of Animal Kingdom. This is for the forms, the bodies in the Time Domain. It is just one Circle because People all belong to just one *genus*" (here she drew a second circle almost the same as the first) -" and only one *species* in that Genus." (She drew a third circle almost covering the first two.) "There were more genera with more species of People in the Past but not in the Present, so I show them as they are now - though the apes are People but not *Human* People.

"However, People have divided themselves into many groups by such little things as the shape of the eyes or the nose, or the shape of the ears, or the color of the hair or skin - all of these just trivial *differences* in the time Domain. Yet these little *differences* have been given impressive names, like *race, nationality, color*, and considered very important and have caused the groups to war with each other for - oh, many thousands of my Revolutions around Great Light."

"Why?"

"Oh, sometimes one group has something the other wants and doesn't have. Sometimes one group feels it is superior and ought to have more than an ordinary share and feels it deserves to take from others. Many reasons, dear, most of them selfish, based on feeling (or wanting to feel) superior.

"Even in their Questions and Studies they have divided themselves on the Mind/Feeling Domain into many different groups, some focusing on the Plants of Plant Kingdom, either now or in the Past; others focusing on the Animals of Animal Kingdom, again either in the Past or now. Still others study Minerals, some study Light, including Great Light and the Lights beyond. They also divide themselves by what they think about Great Light or Great Spirit or Great Human Mind."

"Why? Why don't they study instead how to be nicer People and not tear down Trees and fight each another and all that?"

Dear Earth's soft smile rose within him, sadness in its tenderness. "Dearie, that is an excellent Question, and it is one that People themselves are struggling with. The Answer will not be found in the Time Domain nor chiefly in the Mind Domain. People will be gradually evolving their Feelings and Souls as I continue to revolve faithfully around the dear Great Light, but it may be quite a few hundreds, even thousands of my revolutions, before People manage to see the Circles overlapping as they truly do; one Family of People, one Genus, one species - but many Minds, many cultures, many Feelings, many Souls, all held as Family members in one Great Soul..

"You see, dearie, as Great Human Mind experimented, he chose the brain to be the part be specially focused on, letting it develop quickly, so Mind, operating through the brain, was able to evolve quickly - so quickly, in fact that Self-awareness and Soul also grew, and each *individual* wanted to be recognized a Self, one Soul, and not just part of a large People-mind.

"Are you content to be just part of Big Plant Mind?" She asked the question suddenly.

"Of course! Because I am a part!" answered Twig-mind. "What do you mean, Dear Earth?"

"Just to show you how different People are from Plants and most Animals, dear. Each People (single ones are called *Persons*) each Person feels individual and wants to be valued as a single Soul, and wants to be respected and cherished. It is a deep hunger in each Person. When satisfied, the Person can turn the Energies into almost any fine direction he chooses, but when this hunger is unfulfilled the person's inner starving results in Depression, Fear Rage, Grasping, and all the destructive Feelings of the Lower Mind/Feeling domain. That is where many of the fightings and other sorrows begin."

"Why don't they get together and figure things out like Plants?"

"Is it that easy, dearie? Plants, too, may crowd each other out of a sunny spot, or prevent new plants from crowding them at a place with plenty of water. One of Nature's laws is the one about preserving one's body, 'self-preservation.' Maybe at the expense of other forms."

"Well, it just doesn't seem right, somehow. Things don't seem fair at all - like with that little Tree being starved by the Aphids, who were all growing fat!"

"Some of Nature's laws in the Time Domain do seem harsh, dear. Nature is an Allness. We need to learn her laws and work *with* them, not work against them. Then we'll get along better most of the time, and Nature will let us learn still more about her laws. As for the Aphids, they have arranged their own deaths unwittingly, you know, by over-multiplying and draining the little Tree's Life Energies. Their forms are all going to die as the little Tree withers."

"Well, Moving told me - when my Twig-form was dying, Moving told me – 'These things happen. But it's really all right. Ask Dear Earth.' So I ask you now, *How* is it 'all right'?"

"Dearie, that is one of the very greatest Questions. In the Time Domain dying is as important as sprouting. A *Beginning* tends to *Become*, and then to have an *End*. In the Time Domain this is the wise Law. If the forms that Begin just continue to live, eventually they overfill the Space and crowd and starve one another. So the old forms are allowed to come Down to me so that new fresh forms have Space to be born and live. It is not a real dying, you remember - not of the Mind/Feelings nor of the Soul, dearie. You already know that. It is in the Time Domain only, that things seem not fair.

"I'll tell you more later, dearie. Your Mind/Feelings are expanding fast, and I am proud of you."

Twig-mind was full of mixed feelings, happy that Dear Earth was pleased with him but still having a lot of Questions in his "expanding Mind/Feelings!"

30. OVERVIEW OF THE KINGDOMS

It was a surprise when not long after this, Twig-mind felt Dear Earth's thought welling up inside him, this time like an invitation, not just a response to a call from him.

"Dearie, we need to look at those Circles in your Diagram in a different way. Are you ready?"

"Oh, I'm always ready to hear what you can tell me!"

"Good. Now here are your Circles, see, one for each Kingdom. But I showed you how many kinds of Plants and Animals there were, right? What if one kind of Plant was very rare and had only a few hundred individual Plants growing, but another kind, although just as rare, had many thousands of individuals growing. How should we show that?"

She waited. Twig-mind waited. He expected Dear Earth to go ahead and show him.

"No, dear, it is time for you to begin to figure out some things for yourself. You can begin to answer many of your own Questions, even. This -" (he felt her gentle smile) "This is another step in your Education."

Twig-mind took a while to realize and accept that from now on he was not a mere Listener to Dear Earth but was becoming a Thinker - at her prodding! Yes, a new stage in his Education, for sure!

"Well, I guess we could show each individual as a dot... for each kind and see how many dots were there..."

"Doing quite well, dearie. Suppose we do something like that, and at first show only how many dots there are in each group, or at least in a few that we choose. Just the numbers, right? Here we go.

"Now here are the Trees. We can't count your Tree because his form is Changed into lumber and chips. These are just the Trees with living Time-forms." She showed a Circle with tiny dots. "And here is how many individual Aphids are living." The Circle was dense with dots!

"In the Human Kingdom there are this many," and the Circle had a multitude of dots. "But look at how many Ant-bodies there are." The Circle was black with dots! "And here are the Termites," (another densely black Circle) "and here are the Spring-tails," (a third dense Circle) "and many others among the Insects are like this, out-numbering Human beings by thousands of times. You see, we didn't count size, did we?

"If we take the *size* and *weight* of their bodies into account, the Circles

77

are like this." She showed more Circles, many of them much more dense than the Human Circle. Even the one for Ants - (Twig-mind knew Ants. They used to crawl on his Twig-body when he Was a Twig.) - showed their combined weight to be more than the combined weight of all People!

"A Diagram - it is complicated, isn't it," he sent the doubtful thought to Dear Earth.

"It can be, dearie, but a Diagram does help us to understand things that otherwise seem too complex. As you saw, we can make a Diagram and then make Changes in it to represent different aspects of the thing we are talking about. Now how about a Life-Diagram of you, dearie?"

Twig-mind, astonished and rather embarrassed, kept silent, wondering what Dear Earth had in mind this time. He felt her gentle teasing smile.

"Well, here is Twig." A solid statement: *Twig.* "And Twig grows, produces Buds that grow into Leaves, and then Terminal Bud grows and becomes Terminal Sprout and grows more Leaves." As she created the images from the Past, Twig-mind relived them vividly, joyously, in the Time Domain.

"There was Storm - and the Big Cold - and People came and sawed off many of Tree's Branches and took them away and Twig was torn loose and lay against my cheek..." She paused.

Twig-mind saw, felt, and relived all of this, felt his Feelings again, thought his Thoughts again. He felt Moving brush him softly as he lay. He felt Moving's tender caress, his quiet sorrow: "Sorry, Twig. These things happen. Really it's all right. Ask Dear Earth."

He was looking Down at his Twig-body lying there. He was trying to ask Moving something, but Moving ignored him, seemed not to be aware of him at all. Then for the first time he felt the now-familiar gentle smile within him, Dear Earth's communication, quiet, deep, pervasive, caring.

The review continued swiftly: all his Questions, their Answers, all were open to his Memory, to his Awareness as he focused on each. Suddenly he knew that whatever in Plant Kingdom he focused on was also open to him. He only had to turn his awareness to a certain Tree or Plant or event and *he could feel-into it clearly*, more clearly than if he were right there in the Time Domain!

He turned his Mind to Dear Earth, who seemed to be waiting with a chuckle of expectancy.

"I - I - it does seem wonderful! How do I do it? Are you helping me?"

"Your Twig-Mind has learned much, dear, and now you can control it much better. As you just found out, when you focus on anything, you can be right there gaining knowledge of that thing. This is a kind of Graduation in your Education, dearie. The whole Plant Kingdom is open to you. Congratulations!"

"Well - I - I guess - I mean, Thank you, Dear Earth. But what do I do now?"

"Dearie, now you are free to choose what you want to do, and then go to work and do it. I am always here, but now you will be asking your Questions after you yourself have tried to answer them, and then you'll ask them of Great Plant-Mind, and after that from me. Okay?"

"Ye-es, I guess so," Twig-mind felt rather doubtful. "But what if my Question is about something in Animal Kingdom or Human Kingdom? Or in Mind/Feelings Domain? Or Spirit Domain?"

Somehow the Universe seemed even bigger and more mysterious and full of Questions than he had ever felt it before.

"Ask Animal Questions of Great Animal Mind, and Human Questions of Great Human Mind. Ask Mind/Feelings Questions of me or of Great Light, and Spirit Questions of The Big Holy.

"The Universe is bigger than any of us can comprehend, dearie. I don't know the answers to all the questions, nor does Great Light, and he says that not even Greater Light knows all. The Law about 'Every Beginning has an Ending' is a Law in the Time Domain only, dear. In the other Domains there seems to be expansion and widening, deepening and evolving forever, or at least farther than we are able to see.

"If not, we'll never know," she finished with her quiet chuckle. "We won't be there."

Twig-mind wasn't entirely satisfied. How could she laugh about it?

Dear Earth knew his thought, of course. "Dearie, right now, how do you feel, talking with me? Are you worried, scared, anxious?"

"Of course not! You are here, you care about us all, you take care of us the best you can."

"Yes, and that Feeling of yours is called 'Trust,' dear, or 'Confidence.' They are beautiful Feelings, and those are the Feelings that I have toward Big Holy, who oversees all of us in Great Light's Family. I feel that Big Holy knows me intimately and cares for me as I do you, little Twiglet."

She called him by his Budhood name. It made his mind want to snuggle up close to hers as once he snuggled close to Branch at his Union Place. So this was the way she felt about Big Holy? That she was snuggling up to Big Holy as he, Twig-mind, was snuggling up to her? Big Holy must be truly wonderful and caring.

Suddenly, as he was thinking this, another Sense came into him, not really a Feeling, not really a thought, but Something else, Something Beyond. It was very still, silent, strong, powerful... and very... very wonderful... Twig-mind didn't have any way to express what it was.

"You sense It, dear? This is Big Holy. When It dwells in your mind you become a *Twig-soul* in the Spirit Domain. Now be still, dearie, and let Big Holy teach you. You only need to be very still."

31. THE BIG HOLY AND THE SPIRITUAL KINGDOM

Twig-mind was so overwhelmed again that he felt there was nothing he *could* do but be still! Repeatedly he had come to a point like this, feeling lost in an Expansion! Each time he had felt that he could not possibly stretch his mind and take in more Information, more Education! However, Dear Earth believed that he could... so he could *try* - - No, not *try*, "*just be still.*" Well, try to be still, anyway.

His mind swept back over his life and recalled a time when, as little Twig, he had felt a vast Safety enveloping his world and himself and had peacefully and trustingly let himself sink to sleep in it. He remembered another time when Dear Earth was telling him about Great Light. She became very quiet and reverent when she spoke of Great Light, and Twig had felt her stillness. Those times were a little like this feeling of Presence now.

At first he felt embarrassed, as if he thought Big Holy was watching his mental struggle. Of course Dear Earth was watching he knew, but be didn't mind her. He knew she was sympathetic with his Mind/Feeling efforts and Questions. As he thought this, suddenly he knew that Big Holy was equally - *even more than equally* - understanding and sympathetic. He sensed It right here inside, just as he always felt Dear Earth, *only more so, closer, deeper inside...*

Somehow he didn't have to *try* to be still. He just *was* still, very quiet, as if in a Time/Space that was completely dark and yet completely luminous, totally silent yet full of - what? - joy? - fulfillment? Anyway, it was wonderful.

He felt the sweet soft rustlings of other Plant-minds around his own, he sensed their Mind-souls, (if that was what they should be called) and he felt the littleness of all of them at the same moment that he also felt the importance and sacredness of each one. His mind completely ran out of thoughts to describe all he felt and sensed. The Big Holy was All Around and All Inside. Why, it was like Dear Earth's description of Water-Places, where Fish-Animals swam in the Water, breathed the Water, found their food in the Water.

"Very good, dearie," he felt Dear Earth's whispered thought, or perhaps the Big Holy is like Air Time/Space creatures who breathe Air, live in Air, move in Air."

"What do I do now?" Twig-mind whispered back, almost afraid to lose this contact by so much as a Question or a Thought. "It is Changing me - I can feel the Changing - What should I do now?"

"Just continue to become what potentially you always have been, dearie, continue to let your Twig-mind expand and become the *Twig-soul* you have always been. The lessons in your Education now will concern *Intuition,* feeling the sacredness of all Lives in every Kingdom in the Time Domain, of all Beings in the Mind/Feeling Domain, and of every Soul in the Spirit/Soul Domain. That is a large list of lessons ahead for Twig-mind's Education, isn't it, dearie."

"It - it - How can I ever - ? I thought you said I had Graduated, Dear Earth!"

"Ah, yes, from one Grade to the next, you have, dearie, but there is no end to Expansion, even in the Time Domain. No, dearie, we are all still asking Questions!"

When her thought ceased in that quiet reverence that Twig-mind had felt in her before, he tried to be quiet again for the Greater Awareness. It seemed to be penetrating, permeating, drenching him, and also was within him, radiating out from him, flowing outward into other Mind/Souls, losing Its boundaries (If it ever had boundaries).

Then another Thought came sneaking in, another Question: "I wonder if there is a *Bigger Holy*? A *Biggest Holy*?" Hastily he tried to call back the Thought, to make it *not.* That was so *presumptuous! How could he be so presumptuous as to ask a thing like that of such a Tremendous Being as Big Holy!*

He felt he ought to shrivel up, to apologize somehow, to -

Then, along with Dear Earth's silent laughter at him he also felt an enormous kindly affection: Big Holy was smiling at the presumption of this small Mind/Soul! Big Holy was aware of it, knew of its insistent selfhood, knew intimately of its hopes, dreams, yearnings, strivings, and its fear of being misunderstood - and Big Holy held this small living Mind/Soul in Its great Silence as tenderly as It held Dear Earth herself.

Suddenly Twig-mind was no longer embarrassed or afraid. His love rushed out to Big Holy just as it always had to Dear Earth. He didn't need to tell Big Holy how he had Changed in that instant.

The response of Big Holy in return for his Trust, if put into thoughts, seemed to be something like this: "*I... am... Here... Now...*"

"*I...*" - - and Twig-mind sensed a vast Awareness, a Consciousness that had formed an immense and splendid Plan that included everything in the Time Domain and beyond - every speck of dust, every star and galaxy, every Creature, every Thought, Feeling, Purpose...

"*...am...*" and Twig-mind sensed the Livingness, the Beingness, of every Star and every Creature, and every Thought and Feeling and Ideal of all those Created Beings, even the rocks, the nebulas, the sand grains and dust-motes. They all had Life, Livingness.

"*...Here...*" and into Twig-mind came rushing all the Distances and Far-off-nesses of the Time Domain and the Mind-Feeling Domain, into a dense, wondrous Singularity of *Here*.

"*...Now...*" Past and Present of the Time Domain came rushing together into this intense immense Instant of *Now*.

All this was flashed into Twig-mind's awareness in the great Stillness. It seemed that a reverse change occurred at the same moment; that his Mind had become stretched outward until it was just a part of Big Holy and lost all its boundaries! This must be a *Twig-Soul...* or... What? If he had no boundaries?

As he felt this, his Mind suddenly felt itself tightly enfolded again by the Bud-scales that had protected him as a tiny Bud... the Bud-scales now dry and loose, content in knowing that their purpose been accomplished... now they were being pushed away from their Union Places and were falling to Dear Earth to become part of her, leaving the living Bud free to expand and grow... and to Become what ever his Potentials were... And to repeat the changes, along with the Changes in the other Domains. And all other Buds, and Nebulas, are following this same sequence: "Littles to Bigs and Bigs into Littles..."

"Do you feel the Plan?" whispered Dear Earth's thought within him. "It means that those Questions we can't answer yet, those things that don't seem fair, even *those* will somehow be worked out in the Plan. Many of the unfair things are caused by the *unwise Choices* of Creatures who have been given the wonderful but grave gift of *free-will*. Many Choices are due to *Ignorance, simply not-knowing-yet*. Some are due to *Mistakes in Judgment*. Others, it is true, are due to *deliberate Malice*. All these will *change.*"

"I don't know all the Answers that you want, dearie. All things will somehow be mingled so as to work out for good in the Great Plan. For now we only need to do our best, and *Trust*. Now we are very still..." She paused.

"Can you feel the Trusting, dear?" She paused again, and the Stillness enveloped them both.

"So our Education continues forever, in the safe embrace of Big Holy. And isn't that *wonderful*, dearie?!"

Twig-mind seemed to be far away, or else deeply inward.

"Dear Earth? Does Big Holy think? Does It Talk? I mean - I think Big Holy is telling me... that It hears Questions... or *feels* them... like maybe Itches or something... and has all the Answers... and when a Tree-mind or somebody's mind asks a Question... Big Holy drops the Question into the Mind/Feeling Domain... and the Answers, too, and they go out all through the whole Mind/Feeling domain... and every Mind that *has* the question begins to watch for an Answer... and when the Mind feels like sort of an *Itch* and looks for an Answer, then it *gets* the Answer that Big Holy sent out... and then the Mind feels happy, Like laughing, or like skipping and singing..."

"Dear Earth, is this the way Big Holy talks? I think Big Holy really *is* here! Really and Truly! I guess Its Place is *Every-Here*, isn't it! Oh, this is *nice!*"

"Yes, dearie, you are contacting and describing the *Intuition Domain*, which is beyond or 'higher' than the Mind Domain. And Big Holy really and truly IS 'Every-Here,' just as you said..." She paused, chuckled.

"Somehow I wouldn't have thought of calling an *Inspiration* an Itch... but *you are getting it*, dearie."

AFTERWORD

Dear Twig-mind,

Please thank the following Trees for their assistance in my writing your story:

- *The big Poplar Tree that we called our "Pet Tree" when my sister and I were children.*
- *The Juniper Tree with a Green Bench to cover the stubs of Branches that had been broken off.*
- *The Big Cottonwood Tree that dropped both living and dying Twigs, and taught my Children.*
- *The young Birch Tree in Casper, Wyoming, and the little Willow Tree in Cedaredge, Colorado, both of them terribly infested by Aphids. Willow Tree withdrew her Life Forces. Birch Tree was cleaned of Aphids as much as possible. Not known whether she survived.*
- *The big Cottonwood Tree in Durango, Colorado, that is so lopsided after heavy pruning, and the Cottonwood Tree nearby that was sawed off at ground level and taken away.*
- *The Aspen Trees that supplied Twigs and Buds for several seasons of Observation and Thought.*

In the Human Kingdom, dear Twig-mind, I want us to thank from the Ninetheenth Century:

Ralph Waldo Emerson, Henry David Thoreau, Rudyard Kipling and the poets Walt Whitman and Ella Wheeler Wilcox;

and from the Twentieth Century:

Harry A. Ireland, Agriculturist; T. D. A. Cockerell, Entomologist; Christianna Smith, Geneticist; and Harlow Shapley, Astronomer.

Those whose Thoughts helped me to describe your stages of Education include not only those mentioned above, but also Jeshua of Nazareth, Saul of Tarsus, H.P. Blavatsky, Rabindranath Tagore, Thich Nhat Han, and many others.

I learned to contact the Past as you did, dear Twig-mind, and to think-into and feel-into other Minds and Feelings, by the methods of hypnotic regression and channeling. There are other methods, too, many Human Beings are coming to understand Dear Earth and the other Kingdoms better. Many of us are trying to help Dear Earth now.

So here is your story, dear Twig-mind, a composite but basically a true one. Did I get it, Twig?

Signed,

Louise-Mind
February 2004

www.ingramcontent.com/pod-product-compliance
Lightning Source LLC
Chambersburg PA
CBHW060134260626
47160CB00005B/2101